TO FORGET THE PAST

Tessa Robson is stunned to meet a man she hoped never to see again, but living in a nearby cottage on the estate, meeting Josh Maitland is unavoidable. When Tessa learns of his wife's death and that he is the father of a little boy, she relents, becomes a friend and then loves Josh and James. However, whilst shopping in Newcastle, she is incensed to see Josh kissing a redheaded female . . .

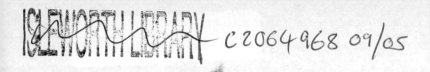

PIA WALTON

TO FORGET THE PAST

Complete and Unabridged

LINFORD
Leicester

First published in Great Britain in 2002

First Linford Edition
published 2005

British Library CIP Data

Walton, Pia
    To forget the past.—Large print ed.—
Linford romance library
1. Love stories
2. Large type books
I. Title
823.9'2 [F]

ISBN 1–84395–863–5

Published by
F. A. Thorpe (Publishing)
Anstey, Leicestershire

Set by Words & Graphics Ltd.
Anstey, Leicestershire
Printed and bound in Great Britain by
T. J. International Ltd., Padstow, Cornwall

This book is printed on acid-free paper

1

It was one of those warm days in April, 1995, without even the gentlest breeze to ruffle as much as a leaf at the top of the tallest trees on the Denton Park Estate. The recent bitter, cold north-easterly winds had relented at last, giving Tessa Robson the opportunity to enjoy a walk and see the parkland beginning to look fresh and green and bursting with life in the bright spring sunshine.

Passing the five oaks, she neared what had been Annie Hudspeth's cottage. Sadly empty now that she was no longer with them, her very old and feeble friend hadn't found the strength to overcome her final struggle with pneumonia some years ago, but Tessa thought of how she could have confided in Annie. More a friend to the whole family than an employee, she had always been there to wipe away childish tears, listen to problems and bring a smile back to the gloomiest face. Annie would have been just the person with whom to talk over her problem, Tessa mused.

Unfortunately, there was no-one to help her today. This was one difficulty she had to work out for herself, she decided, continuing her walk towards her favourite spot where she could be sure of being alone, listen to birdsong and the wash of the river over water-polished pebbles. Her mind focused on devising a foolproof plan of action.

She was well aware that it would take some careful figuring out, just as surely as she knew the crux of the matter stemmed from when she was sixteen. Back then, how she wished she was like Melanie, going on eighteen, old enough to drive, to do just about anything she liked, but Melanie wasn't answerable to her father who, only the day before had embarrassingly referred to her as teetering on the brink of womanhood.

While she had laughed at the time, she had nonetheless objected, had wanted to say his daughter wasn't teetering on the brink of anything, that she was a woman, albeit young, but a woman and most certainly not his little girl any longer.

'Parents! Who would have them,' she mumbled.

But she loved hers and that was half the trouble, never having told them a deliberate lie, she didn't want to deceive them now, but how could she satisfactorily explain an impromptu jaunt into Newcastle tomorrow? Her father was the stumbling block, would want to know the ins and outs of her spur-of-the-moment decision. His all-seeing, police-trained eyes would want a plausible explanation why a girl with tonsillitis would suddenly want to go to Newcastle on a Saturday morning for no special reason.

There was a special reason, however, but that was the other half of the trouble.

'So this is where you're hiding? I've been looking all over the estate for you,' Melanie had shouted as she ran towards her friend, pink-faced, her mop of honey-coloured curls bouncing. 'Have you told them yet?'

'Not yet, but now you're here, we'll go back to The Hall together and break the news but not the whole story, Mel, just that we're going into Newcastle tomorrow and staying overnight with Grandma, nothing more,' Tessa warned. 'You know my father. If he suspected for a minute where we were going tomorrow night, he'd instantly put the kibosh on our plans.'

'If you're really worried about this, I could go on my own. After all, Tess, you're still full of antibiotics after your tonsillitis and you do look quite pale,' Melanie said, her brown eyes showing concern.

'Well, that's only to be expected, but you know me. I always bounce back and you can't go alone, Mel. This is the big break you've been looking for and it's such a brilliant idea. I'm surprised you haven't thought of it long before now.'

'There has to be more to life than reporting on births, weddings and funerals and I would appreciate your company, Tess. It's quite a scary project and while I've heard it gets crowded on Saturday nights, that's where I'll get the latest info for my big story. I'm confident it'll work and with my first real piece of investigative journalism, old Willoughby is bound to be impressed and offer me a part-time job on the Mercury while I'm at Newcastle University.'

*   *   *

Sally looked at her daughter, thought she looked pale, but her temperature was normal. Then again, she had a naturally pale complexion and always was willowy. And when had her lovely eyes, very long, thick dark hair and her very femininity not made her look incredibly vulnerable, as if a puff of wind would blow her over?

Sally smiled thinking of how Tessa's appearance belied her strength of character and anyway, she couldn't keep her cooped up for ever.

'As long as you feel all right, Tessa, I think an outing to Grandma's will be a nice change for you. The weather's warm and you'll come to no harm with Melanie.'

'Where's Daddy?'

'He left for London after breakfast for a special agricultural meeting. Said he'll be back sometime on Sunday, depending on the traffic.'

Tessa glanced at Melanie, raised her eyebrows heavenward, scarcely believing her good luck at escaping the police inquisition.

'Great, Tess. I'll call for you tomorrow morning and we'll be in Newcastle in good time for lunch with your grandma. See you,' Melanie said casually, leaving the drawing-room, figuring Tess wasn't the only one having difficulty in controlling growing excitement at the project.

'Your Uncle Harvey and Aunt Emily will miss Mel when she goes to university. Calvert, Mel and you seem to have grown up so quickly.'

'I know you miss, Cal, Mummy, so do I, but there's a chance that once he comes down from Oxford he'll set up his own law business in King's Denton or perhaps become a partner in Uncle Harvey's law firm, in which case he would live here again,' Tessa said optimistically, wanting her mother to look on the bright side when, in all honesty, she suspected any chance of that happening was virtually nil.

'I doubt if your brother will be happy settling in a small market town after his years at Oxford, Tess, but that's what your father and I are hoping for.'

And that's precisely what Melanie Sinclair is hoping will happen, but Tessa knew that Calvert was having the time of his life at university and not thinking seriously about Melanie or any other girl, certainly not contemplating a steady relationship, she was absolutely sure.

'Don't worry, Mum, I'm still here and will be for the next eighteen months if you can bear the thought,' she said, making her mother laugh.

And whilst there was a strong, family resemblance between her and her brother, the difference in their natures was poles apart. She had always known that she wanted to study art, whereas Cal had been happy to sail along, constantly chopping and changing his mind about a career, making everyone twitchy and only deciding on law at the last possible moment.

Like Melanie, she would go to Newcastle, do her three-year-art stint there and with Grandma's help, follow it with a year in Paris.

It was late afternoon and Tessa was daydreaming, gazing from her bedroom window across the wide expanse of parkland at the familiar view she loved, telling herself that no matter how beautiful Paris was, she would miss this, each old tree, every blade of grass covering the gently-rolling land stretching away to the river.

Quietly opening the door, Sally smiled at her daughter curled up on the window seat.

'Good, you're resting.'

'I was thinking that Daddy must be the luckiest man on the planet to have been left all this,' Tessa said, raising her hand to the window.

'I've always thought so, but then Cecilia Calvert-Denton had no family to leave The Hall or the land to. She admired and respected your father and saw how diligently he kept a weather eye on the estate.'

'But to be a policeman with no family connection whatsoever to the Calvert-Dentons is so bizarre, a kind of rags-to-riches story.'

'Sort of, but that sounds too easy when the truth is it has taken a lot of years of very hard work. This place was in a seriously rundown state and there was little money apart from your father's pay as a police inspector in those days. We worked non-stop for years to bring old Cecilia's home back to something of its former character and that's all Cecilia asked of your father when she left him the property.'

'I'm glad she did. It's the loveliest house in King's Denton.'

'I do agree, but then you know I'm prejudiced,' Sally said with a broad smile. 'Come downstairs and we'll have an early dinner, just the two of us.'

'And you really mean it about Mel and me going into Newcastle tomorrow? You won't worry about me?'

'What could there possibly be for me to worry about, Tessa? You'll be seventeen before you know it and a more level-headed, self-contained young woman I have yet to meet.'

'Yeah, but not Dad. I wish he would get real. To him I'm still a child without an ounce of commonsense or a serious thought in my head.'

Sally smiled.

'You have to make allowances, Tessa.

10

He's your father, wants to be needed and still wants to protect you. I suspect he's not quite ready to face the fact there could be another man in your life one day.'

The buzz of excitement Tessa woke with the following morning lasted throughout the rest of the day and when later she pecked her grandma's cheek, if her conscience pricked slightly at saying they'd be back soon when, realistically, she hadn't a clue, it was a price worth paying for Mel landing a job on the King's Denton Mercury. And where was the harm in waiting to explain everything to her grandma tomorrow once Mel had done the rounds of the wine bars and pubs in the Bigg Market?

Their first surprise was the Bigg Market itself, how busy it was. The milling crowds of young people were obviously dressed in their best for an evening out and making Tessa regret wearing jeans and denim jacket. Mel looked no better in her grey trousers and pink shirt.

'D'you get the feeling we're slightly underdressed for this gig, Tess?'

'Yeah. More in the King's Denton pub mode than for this Newcastle night scene,' she answered, following her friend into a pub and joining two other girls at a small table.

Mel questioned them on their evening out without much success, then moved to another group, this time of four young men who were much more co-operative, surprisingly honest and straightforward about their drinking and smoking habits.

Tessa was astonished at Mel working the pubs, firing questions then quickly moving on to another group, extracting the information she wanted. Tessa was also impressed at her professionalism. What seemed to Tessa like hours later, in another smoke-filled, noisy pub lounge, Mel bought drinks at the bar and at an out-of-the-way table, was busily writing notes when Tessa said, 'I feel hot, Mel.'

'Don't worry, Tess, I'll be finished soon, so hang on here. I've had a tip about a pub near the quayside, but I'll be back in ten minutes.'

The pain in Tessa's throat had completely gone, but she suspected her temperature was shooting up again and, slipping off her jacket, she laid it on a chair, took a long drink of her iced tonic water and wished Mel would hurry back. Her head was hot, as if her temperature was playing her up again, but Mel would be back soon and if she sat here quietly with her cool drink the wooziness would go.

She looked at the garish, brightly-lit bar and, desperately wanting to lie down somewhere, the lights began to flicker, dim, and as they merged into one, she felt herself falling . . .

For some incomprehensible reason, Tessa felt reluctant to move in the fusty, over-heated, under-ventilated atmosphere as she tried to collect her wits, and getting her sluggish brain into gear was another problem.

Like a strong, wax polish, the scent of lavender drifted and there was a glimmer of light from somewhere nearby. When a feeble attempt to move proved unsuccessful, it became apparent that she was lying on a bed and wherever she was, the absolute silence was ominous. Hesitantly, she wriggled her toes, raised a hand to her forehead, cool now.

'So what am I, Tessa Robson, doing in a strange bed almost in my underwear?' she whispered in a state of growing panic, persuading herself that there had to be a good reason and when her head cleared, everything would simply slot into place, solving the problem.

Turning her head to the right, Tessa saw a pretty Tiffany light on the bedside table which threw a kaleidoscope of colours across the room, for which she was grateful.

Feeling queasy and as weak as a kitten, Tessa eased her legs off the bed, the slight movement making her feel dizzy. Running her tongue over her lips, she wished she had something to drink.

She tried to work out how she came to be in a completely strange bedroom.

It was evidently not a room in her grandma's house or her own bedroom at The Hall, but an old lady's bedroom, judging from the brass bedstead, the pretty lilac and cream patchwork quilt and heavy mahogany furniture.

'No doubt lovingly cared for with a surfeit of lavender wax polish,' Tessa guessed, a smile touching her lips.

Probably the same old lady owner had helped to undress her so what was there to worry about? Nothing disastrous had happened. It wasn't as if she had been kidnapped. An involuntary shiver rippled down her spine at the thought of her parents receiving a phone call for ransom money and their reaction. Her ex-detective father would soon have the police combing the countryside for her.

'And if anyone can find me, he will,' she whispered, a prickle of tears stinging her eyes as she walked across the room and lifted her clothes off the back of a white wicker chair.

Jeans, T-shirt, jacket, shoes and the emerald green silk scarf she had borrowed from her grandma to tie back her hair, they were all there. How long had she been here and why was she feeling so muddle-headed?

Pushing aside one of the curtains, she saw it was dark, but the street lights had not been switched off, so it couldn't be very late, she reasoned, and the house must be occupied for it to be so ominously silent, yet there was a shaft of light from the partially-open door, either from the upstairs landing or another bedroom perhaps.

Thankful that her headache was lessening, Tessa pulled on her jeans and T-shirt, memory flashes and chaotic thoughts tumbling over themselves as she tried to recall exactly what had happened. Trying to piece together odd, fragmented scenes or snatches of conversation, she recalled a man looking at her, a tall, eccentric-looking individual wearing a sandwich board bearing the words, 'Repent, the end of the world is nigh.'

Laughter bubbled at the offbeat recollection which Tessa immediately tried to stifle, trying to make no sound at all until she was safely out of this house and could discover where she was. Glancing in a tall mirror fitted in the door of an intricately-carved wardrobe she was shocked at her appearance. Her eyes were too big for her unusually pale face and her mass of tangled luscious hair looked like a veritable bird's nest.

'It really is time you did something about that mop, Tessa Robson,' Melanie had said before they left for the Bigg Market to get her story.

Tessa had felt duty bound to help her. This wasn't one of Melanie's run-of-the-mill jobs, but an on-the-spot exposé of drink and drugs in the teenage population and important, ground-breaking stuff for Melanie who, while she had not specifically been asked to do it, saw this as her last chance to impress Keeble Willoughby with a serious piece of investigative journalism before she left for university. Tessa was convinced that when she wrote her story and gave it to him, he would see she was resourceful, a talented, committed journalist and he would give her a job on the paper.

'Well, Mel might've landed her story, but somehow I've managed to get myself in this mess and my father isn't here to get me out of it this time,' Tessa told herself dolefully, lifting her shoulder bag off the chair, checking to make sure her purse and keys were inside.

Whoever the woman was, she had put her in a warm, comfortable room and it wasn't as if she'd been physically hurt in any way, apart from the humiliating discovery that a complete stranger had undressed her. That apart, her headache had gone but where was she and why?

Calculating there could be nothing to stop her simply leaving the house, she picked up her shoes, slung her bag over her shoulder and tentatively edged the bedroom door open an inch or two. Concentrating almost all her attention on easing an aperture just wide enough to slip through, quietly getting out of the house and making a run for it, she saw a man's foot and her heart plummeted as she stood, rooted in the doorway.

Holding her breath, she raised her eyes to see a complete stranger sitting outside the door and reckoned the hammering of her heart must be loud enough to wake him at any moment. He was tall, judging by his long, outstretched, denim-covered legs that made quite an effective barrier and Tessa was more determined than ever to get away from this house. Thankfully, her dark-haired jailer was still sound asleep, his head rested against the wing of a high-backed armchair.

Carefully measuring her every move- ment, she stepped soundlessly over the human barricade fearing her thumping heartbeats would waken him, telling herself that all she had to do now was negotiate the stairs, pray they didn't creak, get out of the front door and run as fast as her legs could carry her. Tightening the hold on her shoes with one hand, the fingers of the other curled round the bannister rail, Tessa took her first faltering step downstairs.

Miraculously, or so it seemed to her frayed nerve ends, her feet touched the bottom step without waking her guard. She sighed with relief for that, and for the fanlight above the door and the street lamp giving enough light for her to slip on her shoes. Silently turning the key in the door, Tessa stealthily left the house, pulling the door shut behind her.

Without knowing which direction to take, her only thought was to put as much distance as she could between that man and herself and return to the safety of her grandma's home.

Going in the direction of the brighter lights of a T-junction, sign-posted, she hoped, her mind was still on the man who had looked harmless enough slumped in that chair outside her door, yet his objective was obviously to hold her prisoner in that room, she thought angrily. If he was the only person in that house, the possibility that it was not a sweet old lady who had undressed her and put her in that bed dawned on her.

'How dare he do that to me,' she cried angrily.

Painfully out of breath, she reached the main thoroughfare, stopped, looked round and gave a gasp of relief, recognising where she was. The sight of each familiar building loosened tears she had kept in check throughout the whole frightening ordeal of her incarceration in that house.

'My parents must never hear of this night,' she swore solemnly as she hurried along the near-deserted road.

She was already feeling safer as she pushed on, feeling less sorry for herself with every step, now just three or four streets away from where her grandma and Melanie would be snuggled up in their warm beds. The other encouraging thought was that the chance of ever coming into contact with that man again had to be virtually non-existent.

With cold, shaking fingers she found her key, opened the door and as quiet as the proverbial mouse, she crept upstairs to her bedroom, switched on the light and shut the door with an overwhelming feeling of relief. Catching a glimpse of her clock by the bedside, she saw it was twenty past one and was banking on her grandma being fast asleep when Mel arrived home late and she would assume I would be fast asleep in my bed, too.

'So no-one will have missed me.'

No sooner had she murmured the words than there was a soft tapping at her door and when Tessa opened it, she smiled guiltily at her friend.

'Tess, whatever happened? You look shattered. Where did you go? I've looked everywhere for you,' Mel whispered anxiously.

'I didn't feel well, but I'm fine now and nothing happened, so calm down. It's a long story, Mel, so go to bed before we wake Grandma and I'll tell you all about it tomorrow.'

'Right, I'll go, Tess, as long as you feel all right now.'

Pulling off her damp clothes, Tessa climbed into bed and heaved a grateful sigh. Impressed on her mind was the young man's pale complexion and the stubble-darkened face. Casually dressed, it occurred to her that he looked more like her brother than any kind of criminal, the difference being that Calvert wouldn't dream of kidnapping a girl.

Sleepily, she pulled the duvet high under her chin, promising herself that the dark-haired stranger's face was one she would never forget.

2

It was seven years on, as Josh Maitland slowed his old Morgan as he neared the imposing gates of his friend's home. He stopped, switched off the car engine and pushed the car door wide, anticipating at least a gentle breeze, but was surprised at how absolutely still the air was this morning.

Folding back the car's soft top, his eyes roamed leisurely from the black and gold iron gates standing open as if to welcome him to the charming little gatekeeper's cottage. Looking away, his eyes followed the line of mature trees flanking the drive and he saw The Hall.

Josh gave a long, low whistle of appreciation on seeing Cal Robson's home for the first time, instantly impressed by the fine, old house, but more so by the natural beauty of its surrounding parkland. Walking on, he found himself speculating on a man wanting to work in a quiet environment needing to look any farther than this haven of perfect peace and tranquillity. Living in a cottage here would be more than he had dared hope for.

Still deep in thought, he strolled back to the car, started the engine and slowly moved up the drive before stopping outside the stone-pillared portico of The Hall.

'You'll be Mr Maitland. We were expecting you and if you come into the hall, I'll find Mrs Robson for you. I'm Molly Howard, the housekeeper.'

Josh smiled at Molly Howard as he pondered on the contrast of King's Denton, a pretty little market town, and Newcastle, his own noisy city with its continual vibrant buzz of activity. Although only a few miles apart, they were polar opposites, and by offering him Briar Rose Cottage on this quiet, privately-owned estate, his friend, Cal Robson, was doing him an enormous good turn.

'Mr Maitland, Calvert has told me so much about your university days, I feel we've already met,' Sally Robson said as she hurried into the hall, a warm smile on her face.

Josh took her outstretched hand in his.

'How d'you do, Mrs Robson?' he said, the mother and daughter likeness striking him forcibly.

The lady's hairstyle was that of a more mature woman, but a similar colour to Tessa's long, lustrous raven-black hair that he remembered vividly, and her eyes, they were that same, clear blue-grey.

'Please join us in the drawing-room. We were just about to have coffee, Mr Maitland.'

'Josh,' he said, smiling at his friend's mother.

'Josh,' she echoed with a nod, returning his smile.

It looked as if his friend had it made, Josh thought. A partnership in a local law firm, a majestic Georgian pile for a home, but more important than any of that by a long shot, Calvert Robson had a family.

'I called to tell you what was happening about the removal people,' he said. 'The men have promised to bring my furniture tomorrow afternoon, but of course I'll be here, waiting at the cottage for them, so the family won't be disturbed in any way.'

Josh felt it was his duty to explain before they joined the others in the drawing-room.

'That is thoughtful of you, Josh, but you're going to disturb this family more if we can't help you move in. Not only have we talked of nothing else for days, but our working overalls are ready and if Mrs Howard spends any more time at that window looking out for your removal van, I swear she'll take root.'

Calvert overheard his mother's remark and laughed.

'The women won't be much help with your grandmother's heavy furniture, but I've roped a hefty stable lad in to help us, Josh, so an extra three strong men should be enough for the job.'

'Tessa will be disappointed at not being here in time to help Josh move in, won't she, Calvert?' Sally said.

'She'll be too tired to do anything after her long journey from Paris. Who's meeting her train?'

'Your father wants to,' Sally answered. 'Tessa's my daughter, Josh. She has been living in Paris for a year, but is due back tomorrow, and we're all very excited at the thought of her coming home.'

'She's at a school there, I believe,' Josh answered cautiously.

'L'Ecole Nationale Des Beaux Arts,' Ben Robson said, entering the room, his sudden presence instantly sending out a paternalistic warmth. 'And why my daughter had to go there after three years at university in Newcastle is still a mystery to me.'

Josh stood and the two men shook hands, saving Josh from offering any comment on their wayward daughter, the young teenager who had frequented

Newcastle pubs on Saturday nights, unescorted, and drank herself into a state of oblivion.

He had known who she was that night those years back. He had seen her with Cal in Newcastle a couple of times and the family resemblance was striking. That Cal's hapless sister gave such little thought to her safety, exposing herself to every danger imaginable, was starkly brought home to him that night as he had half-carried, half-dragged the insensible girl out of that pub and hailed a cab in the Bigg Market when the silly, young girl must've been still in her early teens.

'It's good to see you again, Josh, and I hear tomorrow's the day for your big move,' Cal interrupted his thoughts.

'It is, and I'm looking forward to living on your beautiful estate and settling down to some serious work.'

'And we're celebrating Tessa's home-coming and twenty-fourth birthday the day after you move here, so why don't you join us all for dinner? There are

29

always too many women on these occasions so you'll help even the score, Josh.'

'You're very kind, but if it's a strictly family affair, I . . . '

'But it isn't,' Sally chipped in. 'Emily, Harvey and Melanie Sinclair are friends, so you wouldn't feel surrounded by Robsons, Josh. We would love you to come.'

Josh looked from Sally's face to Cal's and grinned, raised his arms in submission and said, 'You win, Sally.'

'Mother usually does,' Cal added and Ben burst out laughing.

'Thank you both for your kind invitation,' he said, following Cal and getting out of his chair. 'I'll look forward to it, but first, I'll see you tomorrow at Briar Rose Cottage.'

The two men strolled in the sunlit parkland towards the river and Josh's new home in companionable silence. The serenity of the estate, while thoroughly familiar and probably taken for granted by Cal, was a whole new, captivating experience to Josh who had spent his life, for the most part, in an industrial city.

'The sky looks bigger here and a brighter blue,' Josh remarked, noting the freshness of the air, with birds and the slow-moving river the only sounds to be heard.

'There, beyond the five oaks, is Briar Rose Cottage. I understand from Molly Howard that the chimney has been swept and a load of logs delivered and stacked ready for you. You might find it on the small side, Josh.'

'If there's space for my big desk and bed, the cottage will be big enough for me,' Josh answered, contented just to be here, to have found somewhere to work in peace. 'I told you roughing it wouldn't be a problem, but to me, that cottage looks more like a desirable residence than the dilapidated hovel you made it sound.'

'Well, it didn't seem much of a home to offer a friend.'

Josh could understand that it wouldn't,

not to Cal. He would see it as just another cottage on his family's estate.

'I'm grateful. When the buyer of my Newcastle house couldn't wait for me to move out, I found myself with nowhere to live and nowhere to work.'

'Well, you have a place now and tomorrow, my sister is in for the surprise of her life when she discovers we have an author living in Annie Hudspeth's cottage.'

Cal laughed.

'When she's here, does Tessa live at The Hall?'

'She has done, but she's going to want a place of her own now. She's a clever artist, dead set on a career and is going to need a studio. Still, I can't see her leaving Denton Park and there are two very good reasons for that,' Cal said, smiling to himself, and when Josh looked questioningly at him, he added, 'She has no money of her own and she loves this place. My sister is a single-minded lady who knows what she wants and usually gets her way, but at heart, Tessa's just a country girl.'

They wandered back towards The Hall with Josh mulling over the possibility that later in the year, if Cal's sister perhaps chose to live in Downey Cottage, also unoccupied at present, they would be neighbours and whilst he could understand her loving this place, the thought of Tessa Robson being essentially a quiet country girl was stretching credibility!

'See you tomorrow then,' Josh said, opening the door of his car.

'And with a bit of luck we'll get a day as fine as this. See you, Josh.'

Leaving King's Denton behind, Josh's mind was still on the Robson family and their kindness to him, but more particularly on Tessa. What had Cal's countrified sister, who had looked about fifteen or sixteen years old back then, been doing alone in a pub in Newcastle on a Saturday night? Discovering more about his friend's mysterious sister would be an interesting exercise.

Thinking of that night, she had

passed him on her way to the front door of his grandmother's house and couldn't have avoided seeing him, but Josh figured it more probable that after six or seven years she would have completely forgotten the incident and while he had not forgotten either that incident or the lovely Tessa Robson, he doubted she would recognise him.

★ ★ ★

Impatiently tapping her fingers on the steering-wheel of her little red Renault, Tessa waited for the lights to change before easing her handbrake off and inching along the Boulevard St Michel, jammed bumper to bumper with vehicles. Their progress was painfully slow today.

'That's where I should be on such a beautiful spring day,' she told herself, glancing from the car window at the crowds strolling in the warm afternoon sunshine.

The pavement cafés were overflowing

with groups of men and women, others congregating to browse at stalls that spilled from the countless bookshops, most of them students from the nearby Sorbonne, she guessed. She was going to miss the art school, miss her apartment on the Left Bank and the friends she had made, but the good news was that she was all packed up after her year in Paris and going home to King's Denton tomorrow. Thinking of Calvert's phone call yesterday, Tessa laughed.

'It's about time you were home, sis. You'll be twenty-four in a couple of days and haven't done a day's work in your life, so get back here before you become institutionalised!'

She was still laughing as she crossed the bridge over the Seine on her way to the station to meet Melanie's train from Brussels. While she was sorry they were not spending more time together in Paris, they were going home and, if anything, Mel had sounded more eager to get back than herself. The reason,

Tessa felt sure, was Cal, her brother. Yet while Mel had always loved him, they remained nothing more than good friends.

Mel knew all about Cal, laughed and joked about his many girlfriends, and Tessa could only guess at how much it hurt her friend and fervently believed her brother's indifference was the main reason Mel travelled the world to report news from some of the most dangerous spots of the world.

While Tessa was full of admiration for her bravery, she wished Mel would find herself something less hazardous than wars and riots to report on. What was wrong with working in a television studio in Newcastle? Reading the news looked a comparatively safe occupation and would certainly be more conducive to living a normal life. Tessa laughed softly, and could almost hear Mel reply, 'But not nearly as exciting.'

It was late afternoon when the girls left Tessa's little car with its new owner, a student friend of Tessa's and flagged a taxi to take them back to the apartment.

'I warn you, Mel, we're not eating at a starred Michelin restaurant tonight, but at my favourite brasserie.'

'Great,' Mel agreed, watching Tessa open the glazed doors of her dining-room, accentuating the sweep of the honey-coloured wood floor.

'D'you realise how lucky you were to have found an apartment like this in Paris, Tessa Robson?'

'I do, but I can't take any credit for it. Grandma has an old friend who told her about it. Gran paid for it and my year at the Beaux Arts, everything, but I'm determined to pay her back when my paintings start to sell.'

Mel gave Tessa an indulgent smile, yet there wasn't the slightest tinge of envy in her heart. Like her own parents, she loved them, the whole family, Tess, her parents and Cal, and as much as she tried to persuade herself otherwise, there was no denying her long-time attraction for

Tessa's big, good-looking brother!

'I was sorry to hear old Keeble Willoughby died, Mel. Mother phoned, and I told her he'd given you your first job as a reporter.'

'Poor Keeb. He told me he'd never employed anyone to work on his newspaper at such a tender age and doubted I was tough enough to last more than a couple of weeks.'

'Well, he couldn't have known you very well, or your penchant for getting into trouble,' Tessa claimed, a wide grin creasing her face.

'I stayed at The Hall that night and Cal pinned the notice to my bedroom door, **Nancy Drew, Ace Detective and Star Reporter**, remember?' Mel laughed. 'Heavens, when I think of those exhausting Saturday nights I spent in the accident departments of the Newcastle General and Royal Victoria hospitals looking for a story. It was such a pitifully sad job I don't know how I stuck it out.'

'My brother thinks I should start

work, Mel. He says it's time I came out of the educational system before I become institutionalised,' Tessa remarked, causing Mel to give a sudden, loud hoot of laughter.

'I'm going to enjoy your dinner party back home tomorrow night. It's been a long time since we've all been together,' Mel said thoughtfully. 'Has Cal found himself a steady girlfriend yet, Tess?' she asked as casually as she could.

'You know him. My brother is found of the female of the species, but has never had a serious thought in his head about any girl,' Tessa replied lightly, bringing a smile back to Melanie's face.

After talking non-stop, bringing each other up to date with their news, Tessa looked at her watch and shrieked.

'Come on! We'd better put a spurt on. It's time we made tracks for the brasserie before the ravenous tourist hordes descend.'

No sooner were they seated at a table in the restaurant when suddenly and without warning, a noisy, fun-loving group of Tessa's friends surrounded them. Pitching her voice above the general din, with a half-apologetic glance at Mel, she introduced them collectively.

To Mel's amusement, she watched extra tables, chairs and huge quantities of food appear as if from nowhere and it was after midnight when the girls dragged themselves away from what had gravitated into a happy, excessively noisy, farewell party for Tessa.

The journey home, first from Paris to London, then a taxi across London to King's Cross and their train north, was long and the girls were delighted when the train finally pulled into Newcastle Central.

'Home at last, Mel,' Tessa said, stepping on to the platform and turning to her friend with a broad grin. 'I told you my father would be waiting for us,' she added excitedly, running full pelt towards him.

'Let's get out of the station and into the car, girls,' Ben insisted, picking up the two heaviest suitcases. 'I'll drop you off, Mel. I know your mum and dad are waiting for you in King's Denton, so we'll go there first. I expect you've been in the thick of trouble in some foreign country and I can't wait to hear your latest exploits.'

'My latest has been eating your daughter's cooking in Paris this week-end. That's quite an adventure.'

'Never mind,' Ben sympathised, 'you're sure to get a good dinner at The Hall tonight, Mel.'

Later, when the initial fuss and excitement of Tessa's arrival home had died down and she escaped to her bedroom, she gazed across the Denton Park landscape she loved, bathed in the pink and golden glow of early evening as the sun began to set. This was where she wanted to be, not necessarily living in The Hall, but in her own place and with the help of her parents and the local bank manager, she would find somewhere on the estate to live and take her first steps towards her career.

When the house grew quieter as the finishing touches were put to the dinner party, Tessa laid out her new black dress with mixed feelings and emotions. In one way it seemed the end of so many things — her education, the carefree days of college and her unbelievably happy year in Paris. Yet looking ahead there were new things, entirely different from the old. It was as if one chapter of life had closed and a wonderful, new, exciting opening lay ahead and she welcomed it, would be single-minded, do her utmost to make a success of her career and grasp with both hands every opportunity her new life had to offer. She promised herself this as she dressed for the dinner party.

The housekeeper opened the door to Emily, Harvey and Melanie Sinclair and Tessa smiled as she came down the stairs to the hall and called out to them.

'What's this? The gathering of the clans!'

As Mel's mother and father laughed, they took a step towards their host and

42

Tessa noticed there was another man talking to the housekeeper. He raised his eyes, looked at Tessa and she returned his gaze then froze. For a fleeting moment she thought she was hallucinating, but there wasn't a shadow of doubt. It was the tall, dark-haired man who had taken her to his home and held her there all those years ago and he was here, in her home!

3

'Ah, there you are, Tessa, honey. It's great having you home,' she heard, knowing the American cadence could only belong to her grandmother, and although still feeling completely bewildered by the sudden appearance of her ghost from the past, Tessa seized on the opportunity her grandma's timely interruption offered.

'It's good to see you,' she reciprocated, kissing the old lady's cheeks, thankful for a few distracting moments to calm her jumpy nerves.

'Who's that handsome young man, Tess? Your latest beau?'

'I've no idea,' Tessa replied dismissively, linking her arm through her grandmother's as the unexpected guest walked towards the drawing-room.

Nor was she interested in him, she thought, not his name or anything about him, except perhaps the reason for his presence here tonight. Whether a guest at her dinner party or not, she had no intention of speaking to him, not after waking up in that bedroom in Newcastle, a sixteen-year-old kid scared out of her wits and him standing guard over her.

Well, she was on her territory tonight, no longer frightened of her own shadow having long since said goodbye to those gauche, teenage years.

'Your father says you could be changing your mind about living in London, and if it's true, nobody could be more pleased than me, honey,' her grandmother was saying. 'And I might add, Tessa Robson, that nobody has missed you more these past twelve months. Come and tell you me what you're going to do now you're back home.'

'That's exactly what I was hoping we could talk about this evening.'

As Tessa and Helen Fenwick walked into the drawing-room arm in arm, a loud chorus of Happy Birthday struck up, the noise just about raising the roof and making her shriek with laughter. At the same time, Tessa was inordinately pleased that after giving a lot of serious thought to living in London, she had finally decided against the idea.

'You look lovely, Tessa,' Ben Robson said, pecking his daughter's cheek and taking her hand. 'Come and meet our new neighbour. He's one of Cal's friends and I've let him have Annie Hudspeth's cottage, so you'll be seeing him around the place.'

'Why here? I would've thought noisy city life where there's plenty of action more a young man's natural habitat.'

'I agree. Most young men prefer city life these days, but this one's an author and he was looking for a bit of peace and quiet for his writing.'

They'd now reached his side.

'Josh, you haven't met my daughter. Joshua Maitland, Tessa. I was telling her you've moved on to the estate.'

His hand was cool, he spoke quietly

and his eyes were deep blue.

'How d'you do?' she mumbled, quickly pulling her hand from his, feeling embarrassed by his presence in her parents' home, wishing him miles away.

'I love your dress, Tess. It looks very French. Isn't it lovely, Cal?' Mel said as she joined them all.

'Great, Mel. What there is of it is a knockout,' Cal agreed, laughing at Tessa before adding, 'It's true, sis, you look stunningly attractive.'

'Now why is it, Josh, that Cal never pays me a compliment like that?' Mel teased.

'I think you look lovely, Melanie,' Cal replied, smiling at her.

Looking in his direction, Tessa's brows raised.

'Creep' came to mind, but she said, 'What is this, a mutual admiration society? Come on, Mel, before we have to return the compliment and tell my brother how devastatingly handsome he looks tonight.'

It was good to be home, Tessa thought for the umpteenth time as she walked into the dining-room and saw the beautifully-laid dinner table. Everything was gleaming, and there were numerous delicate flower arrangements. Her mother's clever handiwork, she could see. But what most interested her was who her mother had arranged to sit next to whom?

'Josh, honey, for goodness' sake, call me Helen,' her grandmother exclaimed. 'Here, look, you're sitting next to me for your sins.'

'It'll be a pleasure and I was thinking that you must've lived in America a long time,' Josh replied.

'Ah, my accent? True, I lived there for many years, but I'm a Geordie through and through, Josh, and I believe you are, too. I'm surprised knowing Calvert as well as you do, you haven't met our birthday girl before this evening.'

'No, we haven't actually met, but I have seen her before this evening and knew who she was.'

Tess hadn't meant to listen to their conversation, but when her grandmother broached the subject of their meeting, she cringed and, glancing across the table at him, told herself nobody could be that insensitive. No decent man would tell an old lady about that night, and how could he possibly know who she was, Tessa wondered.

'Did you hear that, Tessa? Although you two haven't met before this evening, Josh knew who you were. I expect Cal pointed you out to him in Newcastle, probably in your university days.'

'No, it was quite some time before that,' Josh said thoughtfully, glancing at Tessa, who was sure he was playing a cat-and-mouse game with her, prolonging her discomfort, no doubt thoroughly himself.

'How fascinating,' she said casually, helping herself to the roast lamb. 'And how could you know me?'

'The art gallery in Newcastle, Saturday morning. You were with Cal, although more interested in a beautiful pre-Raphaelite painting, I recall.'

'That would be the Holman Hunt, one of Tessa's favourite,' Sally Robson said, joining in their conversation. 'The one she always said she'd give her eye teeth to own.'

With all eyes on her, feeling slightly embarrassed at being the centre of their conversation, Tessa glanced at Joshua Maitland and, grudgingly, smiled. He had turned what could have been a much more embarrassing topic into a light-hearted discourse on her love for a picture and, to be fair, she had to acknowledge that, however distorted, he must have some sense of decency.

Joshua returned her smile, saw she looked more relaxed and also noticed her untouched wine glass, surprised that she didn't appear interested in the wine her father had boasted about putting by especially for her return home, but reckoning she would be on her best behaviour at home. She certainly looked lovely this evening, the angelic look brought out, polished up and worn strictly for occasions such as this, he imagined with a touch of cynicism.

They were having coffee in the drawing-room later and Josh sat beside Melanie who was telling her parents about Tessa's little Renault that was so old, she didn't dare drive it away from a bus route in Paris.

'And that Morgan of yours looks another ancient monument, too, Josh. Is it safe off a bus route?' Ben joked.

Before Josh could reply, Cal said, 'I'll have you know, Dad, Josh's Morgan is extremely reliable. That old car has provided us with many a hasty exit from some tricky situations in its time.'

'Some of the more disreputable events best forgotten?' Tessa said, looking directly at Josh.

'Being gentlemen, I'm sure that Cal and I were always souls of discretion, would never knowingly do any harm, certainly never besmirch a lady's reputation,' Josh said cryptically.

'I'm pleased to hear that, Josh,' Sally Robson said.

'And on that brilliant exit line, if you will excuse me, I'll say good-night to you all,' Josh said, getting up reluctantly to take his leave.

He took Sally's hand and raised it to his lips.

'I can't thank you enough for letting me have the cottage and helping me move in, or for this evening. The meal was delicious, a great evening altogether, and I was delighted to meet your family.'

'See you in the Schooner about eleven in the morning, Josh,' Cal said.

'Always assuming I'm awake, Cal,' he replied, shaking Ben's hand.

'Good-night, Josh. Take care going across the estate to your cottage. It's not difficult to lose your way in the dark.'

'You'll need a torch. I'll get one for you,' Tessa volunteered, rising to her feet on a spur-of-the-moment impulse.

What better opportunity than this to clear the air and let him know precisely what she thought of him at the earliest possible moment rather than letting this ridiculous situation drag on indefinitely.

It was a cool evening and pitch black. Tessa handed Josh her father's powerful torch and had only walked a few yards from the front of The Hall, when she said, 'Well, have you nothing to say to me?'

'I thought it foolhardy of you to leave my grandmother's house all those years ago at that time of night, but I could do nothing about it. I assume that's what we're talking about here? The following afternoon I phoned The Hall and knew you had arrived home safely. Did you find a taxi home?'

'Just who gave you the right to involve yourself in my business? I was barely sixteen, woke up in that house feeling sick and scared to death.'

'And whose fault was that? You were in a pub, obviously the worse for drink. What was I supposed to do? How could I leave you in a place like that on a Saturday night, the kid sister of one of my friends? It would've been criminal to leave you there.'

Tessa stopped dead in her tracks.

'The worse for drink?' she repeated. 'You thought I was sitting in a pub, drinking alone? You can't have a very high opinion of me or my family, in which case, how mortifying for you to have to suffer the hospitality of my parents this evening.'

'Just you hold on a minute,' he said, grasping her arm. 'You were virtually unconscious, too young and vulnerable to be in that place. You ought to be grateful, thanking me for taking you away and into the safety of my grandmother's house. You struck me as a spoiled, belligerent youngster then, Tessa Robson, and from what I've seen of you tonight, you haven't changed much.'

Fuming with indignation at his unjustified criticism, Tessa uttered a terse goodbye, swung round and strode towards the house. How dare he speak to her like that! She was neither spoiled nor belligerent and never had been.

And why should she feel obliged to explain anything about that disastrous evening to him? What right had he to judge her and if they were talking character analysis here, he was no gentleman to speak to her in that manner, she grumbled to herself.

The night air was sharp with only the occasional hoot of an owl to break the silence. Josh turned up his jacket collar, enjoying his walk from The Hall to his cottage in the stillness of the night.

It had been a pleasant evening. The dinner was special and he had met a few interesting people, particularly Cal's friend, Melanie Sinclair. She was a charming, attractive and witty female, but not as lovely or as maddening as Cal's sister, Tessa.

Meeting her tonight after all those years had stirred up some old images, memories of the girl he had instantly recognised as Cal's sister, her young body slumped over a bar table. He recalled how he had half-carried, half-dragged her out of the pub into the pouring rain to wait for a taxi then get her to his grandmother's house to sober up. It had been his intention to take her home after a sleep, but he woke up to find his charge had gone.

She had been completely helpless, looked so fragile, he had been almost afraid to touch her and wished his grandmother had been home to take off her wet clothes. He could not forget how lovely she was and that image had stayed with him for quite some time.

Josh opened the cottage door.

'By all accounts, you're quite a girl, Tessa. Incredibly lovely, a talented artist, headstrong, with a fiery temper. What a perfect combination for some poor, unsuspecting guy to take on,' he told himself, laughing at the thought.

The family was having breakfast the following morning when Ben Robson lowered his newspaper, looked over the top of it to his daughter and said, 'Well, Tess, have you made up your mind yet?'

Tessa knew exactly what he referred to.

'I scrapped the idea of London when I realised how much money it would take to start up a business there, but I don't actually want to leave here.'

'Oh, Tessa, that is good news.'

Her mother gave her a warm smile. So like her father, her daughter's positive approach regarding her future didn't surprise her in the slightest.

'Great news. There's plenty of room for you in The Hall. You can choose a couple of rooms. We can easily knock down a wall, put big windows in and turn it into a proper studio.'

'That's not quite what I meant, Daddy,' she answered tentatively. 'When I said I don't want to leave, I meant the estate and wondered if you'd let me rent The Lodge.'

There was a long pause as her parents looked at her in stunned silence.

'Downey Cottage would be more suitable. The rooms in The Lodge are poky and dark,' Cal reminded her.

'I know the light isn't good enough

for a studio, but I thought I could speak to the bank manager about a loan to build a studio nearby.'

Tessa looked at her father.

'I know I'm asking a lot of you, maybe too much. Is there some specific problem in renting The Lodge from you?'

'I would let you have it tomorrow if it was mine to give, but it's your mother's property.'

Her curiosity aroused, Tessa looked across the table at her mother.

'It's true. I bought that little gate-keeper's lodge from Cecilia Calvert-Denton shortly after starting work at the King's Denton hospital. Mind you, it'll need a fair bit of cleaning out before it's fit to live in,' Sally warned.

'But you'll let me have it? I will pay the going rate for renting it from you,' she said before adding, 'if it's not too much.'

Breakfast ended with laughter ringing round the dining-room, the family knowing all too well how being perennially short of cash was Tessa's biggest problem and an on-going family joke.

'You'd better take a look at it before rushing into anything.'

'Right. If I can have the keys, I'll go there now. You mean it? You will let me have it?'

Sally moved out of her chair.

'Come on, I'll get the keys. Of course you can have it,' she said, secretly delighted her daughter had decided to begin her working life here, no more than four or five hundred yards away from The Hall.

As Tessa strolled down the drive towards The Lodge, the cool breeze ruffled her hair, the drifts of daffodils as golden as the sun, reminding her again of how beautiful Denton Park was in springtime. She was about to turn the key in the door when a voice startled her.

'I was hoping we would meet today.'

She looked questioningly at Josh.

'Yes? I can't imagine why.'

'To apologise for last night if it left you with the impression that I had anything but the highest regard for your parents.'

Josh paused briefly, watched her valiant attempt to open the heavy oak door, then stepped forward, gave it a hefty push with his shoulder and held it open for her.

'Thanks. It has been a long time since anyone lived here,' she said grudgingly.

'I can smell the mustiness. You need to open the windows or you'll soon be choked, and they're probably stuck, too,' he added, following her into a comfortable, well-furnished parlour.

'My mother lived here and the furniture was my grandmother's,' she explained, glancing round, assessing the practicability of being The Lodge's next occupant and instantly feeling confident, sure that she was making the right move.

She glanced at her uninvited guest. She had thought in some detail of what he said to her last night. She had been angry at the time, but today her feelings towards him were ambivalent. He had gone out of his way to apologise to her, and if they were both going to live on the estate, she couldn't harbour a feeling of resentment against him when the chances of meeting regularly were fairly slim, so they should at least put on a civilised show of getting along as neighbours.

'Your grandmother told me you'd been seriously considering working in London,' he said, breaking the silence.

She nodded.

'Either there or here and I settled for the quieter life. I'm going to need a studio to work in, but once this place is cleaned up and some of the heavier pieces of furniture moved out, it should be fit to live in.'

'You're going to live here?' he asked, his disbelief evident.

The idea of a young woman choosing to live alone on the edge of the large estate, with Denton Park Hall an option, seemed crazy to Josh.

'I lived alone for a year in Paris, Mr . . . '

'Josh,' he interrupted. 'Yes, but with your parents living so near, why not stay there?'

'I want to be independent. It's about time I stood on my own two feet and started working for a living,' she said, not really expecting him to understand.

He looked at her — independent and single-minded. Josh understood.

'Well, if you want help to move in, just ask. You know where I live. See you, Tessa,' he said, about to walk out of the parlour.

'Thanks for the offer, but I'm sure you have better things to do with your time. Helping me could prove habit forming,' she quipped.

'You should have a phone installed. You're cut off here,' he said.

Cut off? She had lived on the estate most of her life and heavens, above, what was there to be afraid of — marauding King's Denton natives?

She laughed softly to herself. Joshua Maitland ought to bear in mind that she was no longer a vulnerable sixteen-year-old, but a woman now perfectly capable of taking care of herself.

Tessa strolled into the kitchen and from there gave the bathroom a cursory glance before peeping into the two dusty and airless bedrooms, concluding that her mother was right. Her little lodge did indeed have a charm that was all its own and would suit her purposes admirably.

She heard a car slow down as it neared the main gates and running out to see who it was, smiled at Cal and his passenger, Josh.

'Why don't you and Mel join us for a drink in the Schooner?' Cal shouted.

'I'm busy this morning so don't bank on it,' she called back with a wave, watching the car pick up speed and disappear as it turned into the lane.

Guessing Melanie Sinclair would be delighted with the opportunity to spend an hour or so in her brother's company, Tessa decided to act on her hunch and, quickly locked the door. She hurried across the park in the direction of The Hall and her mother's car.

Calculating the work to be done before she moved into her new home, she reckoned it would take a few days to clean and make habitable, but it looked structurally sound, just about perfect to her and she knew the exact spot for her studio, but needed to talk to her father before enquiring about a loan from the bank to finance her project.

'I'll pick you up at Juniper Cottage in half an hour, Mel,' she promised, putting the phone down and smiling at her mother. 'I wish you wouldn't worry. I'm really happy about The Lodge and there's more than enough room for me if some of Gran's furniture is moved out,' she said. 'Oh, and, Mum, could I borrow your car? Cal invited Mel and me for a drink and I said I'd pick her up at Juniper Cottage.'

'That's nice, dear. Of course you can take the car, and don't you think Joshua Maitland a charming young man?'

'Cal and he appear to be good friends,' she answered obliquely, momentarily stuck for a more straightforward answer.

'Poor Joshua! I'll hurry along and get the car keys for you, dear,' Sally murmured, leaving her daughter staring after her retreating figure, wondering why anyone could think Josh poor.

He looked well-dressed to her, in fact it had crossed her mind this morning that he could be regarded as reasonably handsome by some. He had a fine physique, his eyes were very blue and maybe if he smiled more often . . . then again, perhaps her mother didn't mean poor as short of cash.

Tessa gazed out of the drawing-room window at the brilliant sunlit scene, recalling how her mother deeply regretted being an only child and regarded anyone without at least a sibling or two as worthy of her sympathy and Tessa decided that was probably, in her eyes,

Joshua's great deprivation. Her own impression of the man was entirely different. She saw him as positively relishing his free-wheeling lifestyle and not caring a hoot whether or not he had brothers or sisters.

The hotel in the market square was a lovely, old building, very popular and without doubt the best place to eat in their small market town. No sooner had the girls walked through the doors of the Schooner's lounge bar, than Cal's laugh greeted them.

'I'll get the girls' drinks,' Josh said, getting to his feet.

'A vodka and tonic for Mel and a slimline tonic for Tess.'

Josh assumed Cal was joking and said, 'Are you sure?'

'Well, y'know Tess doesn't drink, alcoholically speaking,' Cal said with a grin. 'She never has.'

'What would you like to drink, Tessa?' Josh asked for himself as the girls approached.

'A tonic with ice and a slice of lime

for me, please,' Tessa replied.

'Right,' Josh said, mystified, wondering if it was indeed true and if so, how long it had taken her to come to her senses about drinking alcohol.

'Hi, gorgeous,' Cal quipped, pecking Mel's cheek.

'He says that to all the girls, Josh, usually when he can't remember their name,' Mel explained, showing great forbearance.

When Josh laughed at Cal's and Mel's witty double act, Tessa wondered again what her mother had meant. Poor Joshua certainly wasn't a tag that fitted this good-looking, leather-jacketed man with a pint glass in his hand, laughing at Mel's repartee.

'Did you know Tess is moving into The Lodge, Josh?'

'He knows and thinks I'm a fool to move out of The Hall,' Tessa chipped in, watching his face for a reaction, but Josh stayed silent, his thoughtful, steady gaze holding hers. 'A fool and an alcoholic. Isn't that true?' she added, pressing the point.

Knowing Tessa as they did, Mel and Calvert were amused and when their laughter subsided, Mel said, 'Well, Tess, in a way you are a fool. You'll have to learn how to cook for yourself.'

Tessa laughed.

'It's guilty on all counts then, so who needs enemies?'

'I don't believe that to be true,' Josh said quietly.

'Which of my many mega faults d'you mean?'

'I think you're probably innocent on all counts.'

'But how could you, a stranger, know that?'

'I don't at the moment, Tess, for sure, but we can improve on that when we're neighbours,' Josh said, with equal light-heartedness.

Super abundantly confident was Tessa's immediate reaction, and if surprised at this sudden overt friendliness towards her, she didn't show it, merely let the lively point-scoring exchange end there with an annoying feeling that her brother's friend had won by a mile.

Later, after taking Melanie home, her thoughts were not on Joshua Maitland, but plucking up the courage to push her plans along and speak to her father about the piece of land for her studio. First, she needed his advice about planning permission, then there was the cost of her venture into the business world and where the money would come from.

There were so many imponderables, among them the chances of winning her father over to her way of thinking on this project, and by the time she stopped the car outside The Hall, her problem seemed surmountable. As luck would have it, her father touched on the subject after lunch by casually asking her how things were going. Tessa instantly leaped at the opportunity.

'I need some advice on the studio before I can do anything and, well, there's a whole lot of stuff I'm completely ignorant about,' she said, looking so downcast that Ben Robson laughed.

'Bring your coffee into the study and we'll talk about it,' he said.

Tessa might have known her father would do most of the talking, but she had not bargained for him flatly refusing to sell her the land.

'I have a better idea, Tess. Cal will find the right man to draw up your plans for the studio and he'll also deal with the planning application. It's one of the perks of having a solicitor in the family,' Ben added with a smile.

'And if the way's clear and we get the go-ahead?'

'You have no collateral to speak of, so I'll finance the building work and you can get on with your painting.'

Gazing at her father, Tessa shook her head, amazed at his kindness.

'That's an incredibly generous offer, Dad, and I will accept your help, but only as a loan. I don't know when, but I insist on paying Mother for The Lodge and you for the studio,' she murmured, a prickle of tears beginning to sting her eyes.

'Your grandma says you've worked hard this past year, so I reckon you deserve a helping hand, and I'll go along with the loan idea after you've had a chance to settle down after your Paris lifestyle.'

Laughing as she pushed herself out of her father's favourite, well-worn leather armchair, Tessa kissed his cheek.

'You know this means a lot to me.'

'Not half as much as having you home means to me and your mother,' he replied, gently ruffling her hair. 'So, Tess, first things first. How soon were you thinking of moving into The Lodge?'

4

Much to her astonishment, everything that needed doing to make her new home comfortable was completed by the end of the following week and Tessa moved into The Lodge on a wet, windy May morning.

The family had been a great help, particularly Cal who had worked like a Trojan on Sunday afternoon to help her father with the heavier work. After cleaning and polishing until everything shone, her mother and Molly Howard had filled cupboards and the little fridge with enough food for Tessa to withstand a siege!

Becoming acclimatised to her new, very different environment took a few days, but as a prolonged rainy spell gave way to warm sunshine and the cold prevailing wind turned to a gentle westerly, Tessa was impatient to start work. She took a chair and sketch pad outside and had just started outlining her old gatekeeper's house when she heard the car.

'Your mother said I'd find you here.'

'Hi, Mel. Where've you been hiding?'

'London last week. Have you settled in yet?'

Tessa nodded, laid her pad and pencil aside and said, 'Come in. It's so good to see someone. I'll make you a cup of coffee and you can have a piece of my Dundee cake.'

'Don't pretend you've been baking, not to me. You know I'll never believe it, and what d'you mean it's good to see someone? What about your handsome neighbour? Isn't he a regular visitor?' Mel enquired archly, following Tessa into the kitchen.

'If you're not prepared to believe I can bake a cake, you'll never believe this about Joshua Maitland.'

'Try me? What?' Mel insisted, staring at her friend's serious face.

'Remember the night a man took

me home from that pub in Newcastle, when you were doing your assignment?'

'I'll never forget it. I looked everywhere for you and you never again met the man who took you under his wing that night.'

'I did, Mel. It was Josh. He knew I was Cal's sister, took me to his grandmother's house and put me to bed to sober up.'

'To what?'

Mel's laugh echoed round the tiny kitchen, and when it tailed off she took a sip of her coffee.

'Of course, you've told him you were actually ill? You have explained about your temperature, your tonsillitis, that you didn't drink and never have? That you were waiting for me?'

'Why should I explain my actions to him or care what he thinks of me? I have never forgotten how that man frightened me,' Tessa snapped.

'But he obviously saw you were in trouble and did something constructive about it. He took you to his grand-mother's home and looked after you. As you say, Tess, he knew you were Cal's sister and did the Good Samaritan thing.'

'I must admit to being grateful he didn't tell Cal or the family about having met me before, either when or, more particularly, where.'

'Have you seen him since you moved in here?'

'No, but I've no doubt he's in Briar Rose Cottage with his head buried in a computer. Why, Mel? Are you concerned about him, too?'

'Is there something wrong with him?' Mel asked, puzzled.

'Mother called him poor Joshua so I thought there might be.'

'I know Josh lived with his grand-mother in Newcastle, but she died recently. That's probably why your mother feels as she does and perhaps why they've let him have the cottage here. Have you noticed his eyes?'

'He has two and they're dark blue.

He also has black hair, a pale complexion, he's about six feet one or two, long-legged and broad-shouldered and he has a slight scar near his left ear.'

'So you haven't really noticed him then, Tess?'

Simultaneously, both girls burst out laughing, thoroughly enjoying each other's company, as they always had.

'What about your love life, Mel? And don't tell me you're waiting for my brother to settle down or I'll be too old to be a bridesmaid.'

'What about you? Joshua Maitland looks an attractive proposition.'

Tessa looked thoughtful.

'He's a serious-minded type for a man in his early thirties and altogether too quiet for me. I don't know what it is, but there's something about Joshua Maitland I can't fathom.'

'What's to fathom? He seems a pretty straightforward guy to me,' Mel replied, biting into her second slice of cake.

'Why would a man chuck a perfectly

good law career in Newcastle, and bury himself in an out-of-the-way cottage deep in the countryside?'

'You know why, Tess, to write books. He had to sell his grandmother's house for money to live on until he sold his book. I don't think he's unusually quiet, more the solid, reliable type.'

Mel glanced at her watch.

'Molly Howard's cake is delicious, but I must go, Tess. I'm off to Northern Ireland tomorrow to cover some high-level talks which should take a few days, but I'll be back next weekend.'

As the temperature rose that afternoon, Tessa walked towards the river. After living in a big city, she had almost forgotten how idyllic it was here, how clean and fresh the air, how peaceful. Looking across the river to the big meadow and beyond to a line of tall poplars in the far distance, she heard a voice and swung round to see Josh walking towards her.

'Yes, it is a beautiful day,' she agreed. 'Mel said you'd moved into The

Lodge. It must seem strange to you after The Hall.'

'A bit claustrophobic at first, but the change in the weather has made a big difference,' she replied, wondering when he and Melanie Sinclair had met for this cosy chat about her.

'I met her in the bank earlier,' he said, as if reading her mind. 'She was cashing a cheque for her trip to Northern Ireland. But you're sketching and I've interrupted you.'

Tessa looked down at her old satchel with her sketchbook lying on it.

'It's time I was getting down to some work, but I'm enjoying being home so much, just looking around everywhere, that settling down to work is difficult at the moment,' she answered, guessing he had such a low opinion of her he wouldn't understand, probably think she had never done a day's work in her life and was idle by inclination.

'When I was talking to Melanie earlier, she told me how you'd helped her get her first real job with the local newspaper when you were sixteen and how ill you'd been the night I found you. She explained that you'd had a raging temperature that week and were full of antibiotics. Tessa, I don't know what to say.'

'There are times when I could cheerfully throttle Melanie Sinclair for poking her nose into my business,' she started to protest, but stopped when she saw he was laughing at her and it crossed her mind how the combination of denim-covered legs, blue short-sleeved shirt and a happy face could so radically change a man's appearance, make him look relaxed, more approachable, even younger looking.

'Will you accept my sincere apology or do I have to grovel?'

'I'll forgive you if you never mention that incident again to anyone as long as you live. My parents hadn't the faintest idea where I was that night and I don't want them to know I deliberately deceived them.'

'You did a friend a good turn, Tess, that's all.'

'I would like to close the book on that little adventure.'

'Then we will, and start again with you regarding me as one of the good guys and no longer your bitter enemy, huh?'

The sudden sound of her father's voice made them turn in his direction.

'It looks like good news, Tess,' he shouted. 'I've just had a call from Cal. The architect is coming to see you tomorrow about the plans for the studio and the planning officer doesn't see much difficulty about them being passed if they bear some resemblance to, say, an old-style orangery or vinery.'

'Sounds good, Daddy. Of course, he's thinking of the amount of glass, whereas I'm more concerned with the positioning of light. Still, his suggestion gives us some leeway. What time is he arriving?'

'Nine sharp. I told him you were an early riser,' Ben added jokingly.

'Then I'd better push on and get some ideas down on paper fast. Sorry about you having to traipse all this way with Cal's message, Dad.'

'I enjoyed the walk, pet, but it's time you had a phone of some sort.'

Leaving the two men talking amicably together, she sauntered away from the quiet river scene, smiling, recalling how she had once thought Josh a kidnapper about to hold her to ransom. Hurrying back to The Lodge, she could scarcely believe her fertile, teenage imagination, and Mel was right. Although unknown to her at the time, he had been an exceptional Samaritan.

Turning her thoughts to the architect's plans, basically, it would be a large, airy studio and not a glorified greenhouse. It needed to be close to The Lodge with daylight the all-important feature, the glass roof affording maximum light on the north side. Tessa recognised the strict rules governing new buildings near the site of old, listed ones and hoped that between the architect and the council planning officer they would see her new studio would not in any way detract from the existing buildings on the estate.

As it happened, when Cal's architect friend laid the plans out for her to approve the following morning, she was both surprised and delighted.

'But this is perfect. An artist's studio,' she gasped, genuinely puzzled.

'You mean it doesn't look like a vinery? Well, we could be asked to do a few modifications, so don't build your hopes too high at this stage. With your approval, your brother is submitting these drawings to the planning officer at eleven this morning, so we could have their reaction sooner than we thought,' he explained, smiling at her obvious surprise.

'I'm pleased to hear it, Mr Conway. You sound confident.'

'If you'd wanted your studio built anywhere near the big house, now that would've been a different matter and one requiring a search of some depth into the records, but I'm banking on there being no major objection to the plans for this particular building alongside The Lodge.'

'I'll be on tenterhooks until I hear from my brother. But I'm grateful for the work you've done and can see you knew exactly what I had in mind. This means I must buy a phone today.'

'I'm heading for my office now if you want a lift into King's Denton. I must say I'm surprised you're not on the phone. I would've thought it an essential piece of equipment for a young woman living alone in a cottage on the edge of an estate as big as this.'

Tessa jumped at the offer of a lift and quickly picked up her handbag.

'I'm beginning to think there must be something in what you say, so I would be grateful for a lift and will be holding my breath until I hear the outcome of the planner's meeting.'

When the car pulled up outside the architect's office in the market place, she saw the crowded square and remembered it was market day.

'Thanks for the lift, Mr Conway,' she said, stepping on an uneven paving stone, losing her balance and crashing headlong into someone.

'Tessa? Are you hurt?'

Josh stared at her.

'I'm so sorry,' she began, realising whose arms were holding her, completely overwhelmed with embarrassment at falling on him of all people.

The architect was out of the car and at her side.

'Have you hurt yourself? Look, this is my office. Come inside, sit down and rest. That fall must've shaken you badly.

Tessa gave a nervous laugh.

'You're very kind, but I'm really all right and would you believe, this gentleman is a friend of mine?'

When the architect made for his office, Josh released his hold on her.

'How about a cup of tea in the Bluebird Café?'

'I would like a cup of tea, Josh, and do you know anything about mobile phones? You were right, I do need one but know almost nothing about them. I could do with a bit of advice.'

'We'll sort that out later. The main thing is that you seem to be walking all right, so you haven't broken any bones.'

'I'm fine now, just felt shaken for a minute or two and just hope I didn't inflict any damage on you,' she said, unable to hold back a laugh, the image of his stunned expression at suddenly finding a woman in his arms tickling her sense of humour.

'Oh, I'm a big, strong guy and you're a featherweight, but I have to say that picking a woman up in King's Denton market place was a novel experience for me,' he replied, laughing with her as they went into the café.

As usual on market day, the Bluebird was busy, but they found a vacant table and Josh ordered the tea.

'Have you started to miss Paris yet?'

'I miss having a lot of people around every day, my friends,' she answered thoughtfully.

'Anyone special?'

Tessa shook her head.

'You mean a man? I was too busy working for anything more serious than the occasional party. I've had one or two near squeaks, but nothing serious.'

Josh nodded, smiling as he gazed across the table at her lovely face.

'What's wrong with Frenchmen these days?'

'Maybe it's this English girl who doesn't find life in the fast lane all it's cracked up to be,' she replied, wanting to end the sudden personal drift of their conversation.

Josh took a phone out of his anorak pocket and laid it on the table.

'Have you anything special in mind, or is it something like that you're thinking about?'

'If this one works for you, I'll make a note of the name and model. Where can I buy it?' Tessa asked, fishing in her handbag for a pen and paper.

'I could go to Jennings with you to

check out the latest models,' he offered tentatively.

'Would you? And set it up so I can call Cal on his right away, to give him the number?'

'Sure, but what's the rush?'

By the time Tessa had told him about the plans for her studio, they were well on their way to buy a phone, with her gratitude for his help knowing no bounds, thinking how good it was to have a kind, sensible man with her, handsome, too, she conceded, noting he was smiling more today for some reason. Then again, perhaps he wasn't as old as she had at first thought.

Half an hour later, owning a mobile set up by Josh, and her important phone call made to Cal, Tessa again thanked Josh for his help, which he dismissed with a wave of his hand.

'But talking of phone calls, your grandmother rang me yesterday, wanting to know if her three-drawer filing cabinet would be more useful in Briar Rose Cottage than her house.'

Tessa burst out laughing.

'It's news to me. I didn't know she had one.'

'She has, and your grandmother's an intuitive old lady.'

'You mean you want it?'

'I mean, I could do with a filing system of sorts, so I promised to collect it tomorrow morning. Maybe you'd enjoy a trip to Newcastle to see her.'

'I would love to, but you'll never get a bulky thing like a large filing cabinet in the Morgan.'

'She had that worked out, too, and suggested I borrowed your father's estate car, but I'll hire a van from the local garage.'

'Don't do that. I can have the old estate car any time and I'm insured to drive it. What's more, mother's sure to have a load of things for us to take for Grandma. She always does. It's not a problem, Josh.'

'Apparently not,' he said, amused at how quickly she had solved the transport problem.

'But it could be one of those grey, drab-looking cabinets. Do you really want a cumbersome thing like that in Briar Rose Cottage?'

'I wasn't thinking appearances, Tessa, more useful,' Josh replied, glancing at her softly-flushed cheeks and thinking it had been a long time since he had enjoyed a woman's company as much as Tessa's this morning.

It was a warm, brilliantly sunny afternoon when Josh stopped his car outside Tessa's house to drop her off.

'You have a beautiful home,' he told her softly.

Tessa slid him a sidelong glance and nodded her agreement.

'The locals still call this the Calvert-Denton estate. It was the last of that family, Cecilia, who bequeathed all this to my father.'

'Cal told me the bare bones of the estate's history, but I would like to know more about your father's involvement.'

'You should ask him. It was he who

kept an eye on Cecilia and her two remaining servants when the Calvert-Denton money began to run out,' Tessa said, opening the car door. 'Thanks for your help with the phone and the lift home, Josh. Meet you at The Hall in the morning, about nine?'

'Nine's fine with me. See you then.'

She opened The Lodge door, speculating on her new neighbour, the unknown man who had haunted her dreams on and off for years, suddenly reappearing as if from nowhere in this other, distinctly less frightening form, no longer her jailer, but a pleasant, utterly charming individual, a friend of the family, who for good measure, was not only kind, but a disturbingly attractive neighbour.

Pausing on the front portico of The Hall the following morning, Tessa watched her father driving towards her in the old estate car.

'Where's Josh?' he asked a few minutes later.

'There,' she said, spotting him

sprinting through the park.

'Good morning,' he gasped, out of breath. 'I need to buy a new alarm clock,' he said apologetically.

'It's time I splashed out on a new estate bus, but Tessa's used to this one's idiosyncrasies, aren't you, angel?'

'I should be. Will you help me with the two rather large cartons on the kitchen table for Grandma, Josh?'

'You get in the car and I'll get them,' he offered over his shoulder, already halfway through the hall.

They were well on the way to Newcastle when she said, 'You must miss city life with all the entertainments it has to offer. I know my grandmother has the occasional extended stay with us, but she would find living in the country on a permanent basis a real bore.'

'I miss certain things. Living near a big library for my research work is one, but a visit to a theatre or a football match at St James's Park just means allowing an extra half hour or so to travel from King's Denton and I can live with that.'

During a lull in the conversation, he glanced at her, wanted to tell her how lovely she looked this morning in her pale-green dress, her hair like a raven's wing and the delicate fragrance of her stirring his senses and reviving an older, recurring memory of a younger Tessa. She stopped the car outside her grandmother's house, switched off the engine and turning, smiled at him. Josh looked surprised.

'I didn't realise she lived so near to my old place.'

'Not far at all,' she agreed quietly, remembering running the distance between the two houses in the small hours of the morning, and how on that occasion it had seemed never-ending.

She felt the touch of his hand on hers.

'Of course, you would know the distance. You had to walk from my house all the way here, no doubt scared and desperately unhappy, but however badly you thought of me then, I make no apology for my actions that night, Tessa.'

'And I have no intention of ever expecting you to. With hindsight, Josh, I know now you did the right thing.'

Helen Fenwick opened her front door and called, 'What an absolutely heavenly day.'

Flinging her arms wide, she wrapped them around Tessa.

'Oh, honey, it's so good to see you.'

'Hi, Gran. How are you? And I know I should've called before now but . . . '

Helen Fenwick winked at Josh.

'The road to hell is paved with those promises, but you're here now and that's all that matters. Josh, dear, come and take a look at the filing cabinet, then we'll have lunch.'

After carrying in the cartons of what Molly Howard called her goodies from The Hall's kitchen, Josh had no hesitation in accepting the cabinet, his only reservation that of transferring it from Helen Fenwick's study to Ben Robson's car outside.

'I'll help you with it.'

'It's too heavy for you, Tessa,' Josh replied.

'Would a porter's trolley help? There's one in the garden shed,' Helen told him casually.

'A porter's trolley is exactly what I need,' he said.

'Well, lunch first, then we'll find it.'

They were enjoying a delicious ham salad, when Josh said, 'What made you finally decide to come back home after, how long was it in America?'

'Nearly twenty years. The only reason I left Newcastle was for my sister, Caroline, who was alone and in poor health after her husband died. Then years later when I was alone, as much as I loved Georgetown and the dear American friends I had made over the years, I simply wanted to come home where I belong, with my English family. And when all's said and done, Josh, Newcastle is my home town.'

Two hours later, Josh manoeuvred the filing cabinet out of the house and manhandled it into the back of the estate car.

'There you are, Tess, I knew a physically-fit, strongly-built man like Josh would have no trouble getting that into the station wagon,' Helen said authoritatively. 'I could do with him living nearer to me. He's such an interesting young man and I've told him there's a spare bedroom in this house for him whenever he has research work to do in Newcastle for his latest book, poor boy.'

Tessa was bemused at the idea of Josh and her grandmother being on such friendly terms. She knew her grandmother was tender-hearted, always ready to help anyone down on their luck, but Josh? What was it about him?

'Thank you for the cabinet, the delicious lunch and I loved your chocolate cake,' he said, bending to give Helen's cheek a kiss. 'And I promise to call and see you again soon.'

' 'Bye, Grandma, take care,' Tessa said.

'I will. Look after yourself, honey and, Josh, take her away from me before we both weep buckets. When it comes to saying goodbye, Tess and I never fail to make awful fools of ourselves.'

'Speak for yourself, Grandma,' she retorted smartly. 'And I promise to bring your trolley back soon.'

Josh watched Tessa start up the car, saw her lashes were wet and said gently, 'How about me driving you back home?'

'You could lose your licence and my last vestige of urban cool along with it, but thanks for the offer,' she said, smiling through her tears.

'Cal hasn't phoned about the studio yet?' Josh asked, purposely changing the conversation.

'Not a word,' she shot back. 'I thought I'd phone him this evening and find out what's happening.'

'You must want to get on with your

work, but planning applications take time, Tess.'

'What about your work, the type of books you write?'

Tessa didn't attempt to look his way, so couldn't gauge his immediate reaction, but felt her curiosity justified after hearing 'poor Josh' again. How on earth would her grandmother know whether he was poor or not? Yet it was beginning to look as if her whole family knew at least something about him, with one notable exception! Herself!

'I needed a few hours' break away from writing today, but when we get back to the cottage, you can have a copy of my last book. I'll be interested to know what you think of it.'

Murmuring her thanks while feeling a twinge of guilt for prying into his affairs, she continued the short drive home without uttering another word, and after dropping her intriguing passenger and his filing cabinet off at Briar Rose Cottage, Tessa returned the car to her father's garage and was strolling through the park towards The Lodge in the late afternoon sunshine when the unfamiliar bleeping of her phone startled her.

'Yes, Cal, what happened then? They did? They've passed it, honestly? No hiccoughs at all? Oh, thanks a million, Cal. See you later.'

Tessa did a quick about-turn and rushed back to The Hall. Her father was going to be as delighted as she was that the building of her studio could go ahead without further delay. It also crossed her mind that with half the guile of her inquisitive grandmother, she would have got Josh's phone number and could then have shared her good news with him.

5

As May slipped into June, the temperature rose and the days stayed dry and sunny, giving Tessa the opportunity to pack her painting kit, a sandwich, a bottle of water then wave goodbye to her studio builders and their ear-splitting noise, for the peace and tranquillity of the riverside.

Luckily, she had sold the King's Denton Gifts & Crafts shop the idea of displaying six small pictures and had promised the water colours would be ready by the beginning of July, so there was no time to lose.

Unfolding her stool, she sat down, noticing across the river a bullfinch on a hawthorn branch. She started to paint, her concentration total as the pinkish-red of his breast took shape. Suddenly, the sudden, unfamiliar sound of a child's voice penetrated her consciousness and she looked up.

'Look. A boat.'

The boy was small, about five years old, and too near the riverbank to be without an adult, as this child clearly was.

'Hello, stranger, what's your name?' Tessa called to the boy, watching his hesitation before curiosity got the better of him and he guessed there was no harm in inching closer to the lady.

'It's a boat,' he repeated, a plump finger pointing at the upturned wreck.

'My brother's little rowing boat, the Sweet Sally,' she replied with a smile. 'You didn't tell me your name.'

'James,' he murmured, swinging round at the sound of Joshua's voice, his little face suddenly shining with happiness. 'My daddy,' he called, his arms outstretched, joyfully running towards Josh as fast as his little legs could carry him.

Rendered incredulous by the child's cry for his daddy, Tessa watched as Josh approached with the boy in his arms.

'I'm sorry if James has been a nuisance, Tess,' he apologised, his eyes gravely thoughtful as they met hers.

'He wasn't a nuisance, but he was too near the riverbank for comfort.'

'I can see you're working and we have interrupted you. James has been spending some time with an aunt of mine until I found a place for us to be together.'

'He's a charming little boy and obviously loves his father,' Tessa said politely, her sluggish mind still finding the news that Josh was indeed the father of a five-year old boy difficult to accept.

'Say goodbye to Tessa, James.'

She watched as they headed back to the cottage, thinking about Josh, how little she knew about him. He hadn't seen any need to tell her where he had been for the past three weeks, so why explain the existence of minor items such as a wife and son? Yet, whose fault was it for automatically assuming he was unmarried, for looking forward to seeing him again, even admitting to liking him a lot? Added to which, there was the crazy idea she'd had that he liked her.

Well, one way and another he had fooled the gullible Robsons, and if not exactly deceitful, Joshua Maitland was, without doubt, as deep as the ocean. While she may have given the odd, passing thought to marriage since she came home from Paris, what woman in her right mind would want any kind of relationship with such a taciturn man?

She looked again at her drawing and smiled.

'You'll do beautifully,' she said.

The bullfinch had long since flown the hawthorn bush, but she had successfully captured his likeness, down to his little white rump. Packing up the last few bits and pieces of her equipment later, she wondered if she would ever get used to the bleep of the mobile as it went off. She quickly answered it.

'After I've given James his supper and

put him to bed, will you come over, please, Tess? When I saw your surprise, I realised you didn't know about James. I had thought Cal, your mother or grandmother would've said something. You appreciate that I can't leave James in the cottage on his own and come to you.'

Unsure, Tessa paused briefly.

'I'll call about eight,' she said softly, conscious of a vague restlessness.

Whatever Josh had to tell her, her mother and grandmother already knew and he had their sympathy. Had his young wife met someone else and left Josh and James? If so, what a cruel blow that must have been, but it happened, or they could be divorced without another man being involved at all. But with Josh separated from his wife and little James torn from his mother, small wonder mother and grandma felt sorry for her brother's friend.

The evening was warm, humid, uncomfortably so, but as Tessa passed the five oaks on her way to Josh's cottage, she felt a welcoming cool breeze blow across the river and stopped for a moment. Her mind was still on Josh, loath to acknowledge one other possible scenario and face the possibility that he still loved his wife and was perhaps hoping to win her back. He suddenly appeared through the trees, an indistinct, twilight figure.

'Penny for them,' he said gently.

'Oh, it's you, Josh. I'm idling, enjoying the breeze off the river,' she told him self-consciously.

'How are you, Tess?'

'Fine. Hoping to be in the studio before long,' she added in an effort to keep the conversation on fairly neutral ground.

'I saw the builders were working flat out when I came back from London earlier. They're really pushing on with it.'

'That's my father in his ex-chief inspector mode. He's chivvying them, constantly reminding them he wants the job completed before the first signs of cold weather, or else!'

They laughed as they neared his home, the lights from Briar Rose Cottage filtering through the trees, lighting the way.

Joshua made coffee then told her about his trip, how he had done quite a bit of research work, called at his publishers a couple of times, and brought James back in good time to start school in King's Denton in September.

'My father and Melanie's were mixed infants in that school,' she told him, watching his lips twitch.

Tessa laughed with him, at the same time thinking it said something about their friendship when they could still laugh together.

'Years ago, Tess, we started off on the wrong foot and today, when I saw how completely stunned you were to learn James was my son, I was determined to avoid another misunderstanding between us to fester as the last one did and perhaps, this time, entirely ruin our friendship.'

'So James is the reason you left your job to work from home after your, her . . . when she, your . . . '

Josh's hardly audible voice cut in.

'Clare, my wife, when she died.'

Tessa closed her eyes, completely thrown, her earlier, tin-pot theories shattered by those few words.

'Was it an accident, Josh?'

His eyes held hers.

'No. Three years ago she had a brain haemorrhage. It happened so suddenly, I couldn't believe it.'

'I'm so sorry,' she murmured, unable to hold back the tears that sprang to her eyes. 'It must've been a terrible shock.'

Josh leaned forward in his chair and reached for her hand.

'Don't cry, Tess. I have my little boy living with me again and you've seen what a happy, lively child James is. This is a good time for us. We're together now, putting the bad bits of the past behind us and starting again.'

'And with a new career,' she reminded him, wiping her wet face with the back of her other hand.

'Mind you, I had sold my first book before I left my old job, so I had a foot on the bottom rung,' he explained.

Tessa's thoughts raced. James had been no more than a tiny boy, a two year old, and Josh such a young husband to be faced with a stark, crushing situation, and with his life suddenly falling apart, she could only guess at the depth of his distress and wonder how he had managed to pick up the threads of his life. Yet, somehow, probably because of his baby son, he had done so and had since found a degree of happiness.

'It's time I was going, Josh. Thanks for the coffee and if I can help, perhaps babysit for James if you want an evening out?' Tessa offered, hesitantly.

'Thanks, Tess, and to show my appreciation of your kind offer, I'll walk part of the way back to The Lodge with you,' he said, smiling at her in his calm, direct way.

They had passed the halfway stage of

her journey home when she stopped and said, 'James might wake up.'

'You're not afraid of being alone in the dark?'

'Not half as much as James will be. I'll be fine, Josh. You're forgetting, I know every inch of this estate.'

'You're right. Good-night, Tess, and thanks for coming over,' he said, taking her hands in his and bending, he kissed her cheek. 'James said you had a boat called Sweet Sally.'

'After mother, and I'll have you know that Cal broke a bottle of fizzy lemonade over the front of his new boat with due solemnity on the day it was launched and we were both soaked to the skin.'

In the still of the night, Josh's laugh could be heard across the estate.

The following week, long before the builders arrived, the sound of heavy, unrelenting rain woke Tessa, and she looked up at the grey lowering clouds with a relieved sigh at having, only yesterday, completed her commission for the Gifts & Crafts shop.

She was outside the shop a few minutes before nine, waiting for the shop owner to open. This was a first for Tessa and at that moment nothing in her life had seemed as important as this first sale of her work. She was penniless, heartily tired of living off her family and Tessa saw this sale as an opening of sorts, the pointer to a successful career.

'I'm late, but what a morning. Will the rain ever stop? Come inside quickly and I'm so sorry for keeping you waiting,' the owner said as she rushed up.

Then, minutes later, Cress Slater's sharp brown eyes gazed intently, closely inspecting the six small pictures lying in a row on the long, mahogany shop counter, and equally slowly, Tessa's heart began to sink.

'I think my Newcastle shop is the place for these.'

Tessa looked woebegone as she asked, 'You don't like them?'

'Quite the contrary, I think they're

lovely,' the older woman answered. 'In fact I know someone who would be very keen to see them. I think the small boat with the little boy is absolutely enchanting, my dear, so leave them with me and I'll get in touch with you tomorrow from my art shop in Newcastle.'

Tessa scribbled her phone number on a scrap of paper and passed it to the shop owner.

'Thanks. I'll look forward to hearing from you sometime tomorrow.'

Having already prepared herself for the pictures being rejected on sight, Tessa left the shop in a slightly more optimistic frame of mind, despite her awareness that nothing had been resolved this morning. She was having a cup of coffee in the Bluebird Café when, as if in answer to a prayer, Melanie walked in. A smile broke at the corners of Tessa's mouth the minute she saw Mel and her friend raised a hand in greeting.

'Hi. What brings you to King's

Denton on a morning like this?'

'Business. What's your excuse?' Tessa countered, watching her friend pull out a chair and sit opposite her.

'Oh, the usual. Another job done and a few days off. Anything interesting been happening here? How's the family?'

'The last time I saw him, Cal was fine,' Tessa teased. 'But, yes, something very interesting has happened. I discovered a few days ago that Joshua Maitland was married but that, tragically, his wife died.'

Mel looked disbelievingly at her.

'Is that true, Tess? Poor man. What a cruel blow that must've been.'

'Yes, Mel, but we thought he had no family and he has the cutest little five-year-old son, James, who is now living with him.'

'Heavens, there's so much going on here. Who told you all this?'

'Josh did. Well, after I'd seen his little boy, and spotted the remarkable resemblance, he felt obliged to, I suppose, and he told me that night.'

'He visits you at The Lodge now?'

'He asked me if I would call at Briar Rose Cottage that evening which I did for a short time and he told me about his wife, how she'd died and his dilemma about bringing up a small child when he was working as a solicitor in Newcastle.'

'I can see why it's easier for him to work at home. Poor Josh.'

'Not so poor, really. He seems to have put the sad times behind him, and although of a quiet disposition, Josh seems to be quite good fun to be with.'

Mel took a sip of her coffee, glanced at her friend knowingly before saying, 'And it seems to me as if you and Josh are getting along really well.'

'I wouldn't say that, Mel, but if you look behind you, you can ask him yourself,' she said, laughing at Mel's wide-eyed expression and watching Josh and James walk towards their table.

'Hello, James, come and meet Melanie. She's our friend.'

112

James glanced briefly at Melanie, clearly more interested in his surroundings, the café's bright decor, warm, cosy atmosphere and, Melanie noticed with a smile, the big trays of sultana scones, apple and cinnamon Danish pastries and strawberry tarts on a nearby display cabinet. Smiling at James, Tessa turned to his father.

'And as if I couldn't guess, what brought you here this morning?'

Josh laughed quietly and said, 'Desperation. I had to pack in the idea of working on my book this morning and settle for entertaining his lordship,' he explained, tilting his head towards James, whose attention was now fixed on a rosy-cheeked waitress approaching their table.

Tessa ruffled spots of rain off his hair and James looked up at her, smiled, his little hand finding her forearm as Josh ordered coffee, milk and chocolate brownies.

'It's good to see you, Mel. Back home for a few days?' Josh asked.

'And it's always good to be home, although mother swears I only come back for some decent food and a good night's sleep.'

'Yet I've heard you wouldn't want it any other way, that as fraught with danger as your job must be at times, you love it.'

'I'm a realist, Josh. Don't write books and can't paint so there's not a lot going for me in King's Denton.'

Half listening to their conversation, Tessa's eyes were on James devouring chocolate brownies, but her mind was on his father, telling herself they were bound to bump into each other occasionally on the estate or in any small market town. There was nothing either of them could do to avoid that happening, and why should that bother her?

'I promised you a book, Tess. I'll drop it off at The Lodge when I have a moment,' he said, smiling, watching her wipe milk off James's cheeks, the pair laughing, as if sharing a joke.

'Thank you, Josh. Has the rain stopped? I must go. I've a million things to do. I'll phone you tomorrow, Mel.'

Impatient to hear if a decision had been reached about her pictures, Tessa waited in The Lodge for Cressy Slater's phone call the next morning, and had almost given up hope. She was beginning to prepare a sandwich for her lunch when the call finally came.

'The gentleman I was telling you about yesterday is here with me in Newcastle now and we were wondering if it would be possible for you to join us in an hour or so,' Cressy said.

'In Newcastle? Yes, I'll be there,' Tessa agreed instantly, at the same time picturing her mother's car as the answer to her transport problem.

Speed was of the essence, she told herself, quickly changing into her black suit, smart black shoes, picking up her handbag and glancing in the mirror before locking The Lodge door and heading for The Hall.

Twenty minutes later, after explaining the importance of her trip to Newcastle, Sally Robson was as excited as Tessa and not only let her borrow her car, but gave her enough cash to fill the petrol tank for the journey, with the proviso that she came straight back to The Hall and told her all about the meeting with Cressy Slater's male associate.

Looking at her watch, Tessa's concern was getting into Newcastle before this gentleman wrote her off as unreliable, but after parking in a nearby multi-story half an hour later, she arrived at the shop. She was immediately impressed with the premises which were not a bit like the King's Denton shop but more of a modern, sizeable art gallery.

'Thank you for coming at such short notice and I hope the traffic wasn't bumper to bumper today,' Cressy greeted her.

'Not at all,' Tessa replied, feeling slightly flustered, wishing she'd had a few minutes to cool down and get her brain in gear before being thrown into a business meeting.

She glanced timidly at the tall, grey-haired man at Cressy Slater's side.

'This is Tessa Robson, Mr Shepherd. Mr Giles Shepherd, Tessa,' Cressy began, sounding every bit as nervous as Tessa felt.

Mr Shepherd took her hand in his and said, 'Shall we sit in the office next door? I've seen the little drawings you did for Cressida and would like you to tell me something about yourself.'

Obediently following him to a room the size of a cubbyhole, Tessa sat in one of the chairs and Mr Shepherd sat opposite her in the other, quietly assessing the young, lovely, talented woman.

'Apparently, Cressida knows you and your family and she has given me a brief resume of your art education, so I assume the six pictures you did for her are your first attempt at showing your work, Miss Robson.'

'Cressy told me she liked them and I assumed you were perhaps her business partner, Mr Shepherd,' Tessa stated bluntly, more aggressively than intended.

Giles Shepherd smiled.

'I live in London, where I have a gallery. But my mother lives here in Newcastle, so I'm a regular visitor to Cressida Slater's little gallery. She's an old friend. I found your small drawings particularly appealing.'

Tessa stared at him.

'You mean you want them?'

'I'll give you a cheque for them now. You've whetted my appetite. I would like to see more of your work before I go back to London next week.'

Telling herself this was too good to be true and not to get overly excited, Tessa stammered, 'Yes, fine. I'll bring some from home, or perhaps you would prefer to come to King's Denton, to The Hall, or The Lodge. You can also see the progress on my studio, Mr Shepherd.'

'I'd like that, but call me Giles and

I'll feel less like your grandfather.'

In a state bordering on euphoria, Tessa left The Art Shop, a cheque for her six pictures in her handbag and an appointment for later that week at The Lodge with the London art gallery owner who had shown a genuine interest in her work.

It was such an incredibly lucky break, Tessa was still reeling from the shock, having to remind herself of the mountain of work needed to get the smallest collection together for their next meeting if she was to stand any chance of impressing a man like Giles Shepherd.

The warmth of the sun had dispersed the earlier mist by the time she headed for the multi-storey carpark. It didn't surprise her that this main street was busy at that time of day or that, on the other side of the street, she thought she saw someone like Josh in a smart, dark-grey city suit.

For her, it was one of those magic days when anything could happen.

Nearer now, she glanced across the road again and stopped in her tracks. There was no doubt it was Josh, looking exceptionally smart. But she curbed her instinctive reaction to raise her hand in the hope of attracting his attention when she saw the stunning redhead looking up at him, sharing a joke judging by their laughter.

As though transfixed, she stood in the busy thoroughfare, but when Josh put his arm around the woman and kissed her, Tessa was dumbfounded. Josh's interest in the woman looked decidedly more than friendly and he patently didn't mind who observed his public display of affection.

With the traffic lights now in their favour, Tessa realised they would be crossing the road in her direction and, hating the thought of being spotted by Josh, she walked away hurriedly. Driving back home to King's Denton, Tessa's mind was still on Josh, bemused by what she had seen, wondering what this hidden relationship of his was all about, asking herself why she felt so disappointed when, after all, the man was little more than a stranger. He might have confided in her, told her he was involved with someone. That he had chosen to stay silent on the subject was baffling.

'And,' she muttered ruefully, 'it hurts.'

The delight on her mother's face as she listened to her daughter's adventures at The Art Shop went some way to restoring Tessa's spirits.

'Your first sale, Tessa, and you must bring Mr Shepherd over to The Hall. We must offer him lunch. What's he like and how old d'you think he is? It all sounds very encouraging and your father's going to be so overjoyed.'

Laughing at her mother's reaction, she tried to oblige.

'He's tall, grey-haired, charming and about mid forty-ish,' she went on. 'Quite a nice-looking guy but as much as I'd love to, I can't sit here talking. I'll be in my bedroom sifting through my pictures for the next hour or so, and if I could keep your car to take the best of them to The Lodge, I would be grateful,' she said, giving her mother a winning smile.

'I won't be needing it today,' Sally said thoughtfully. 'Look, Tessa, why don't you leave your pictures here in the drawing-room, near the big windows, for Mr Shepherd to get a better view?'

'He'll probably be impressed with the drawing-room, but in his mind's eye, my pictures will be hanging in his London gallery and I imagine that's how he'll judge them, but after his expert eye has gone over them in The Lodge, if he's not rushing straight back to London, we'll walk over to The Hall for lunch.'

Tessa knew her mother was being kind and she didn't mean to hurt her feelings, but she knew this was something she wanted to do herself. She needed the experience of presenting her work to a professional in the art world, and a scary learning curve it was going to be, whatever the outcome.

After scavenging through water colours, pastels and oil paintings for two hours, Tessa packed the few she thought possible into the car. By the time she had transferred her load from the car to the parlour, it was eight o'clock and all Tessa wanted to do was make herself a sandwich, a pot of tea and fall into a large, comfortable chair.

She was on her way to the kitchen when a loud, urgent-sounding rap at her door made her turn quickly to answer it.

'Hello, Tessa. The book I promised you,' Josh said with a broad smile, passing it to her.

'Thank you, Josh,' she said quietly, surprised at his unexpected visit, surprised he was anywhere on the estate and not still enjoying the delights of Newcastle. 'Please, come in. Where's James?'

'Molly Howard baked him some gingerbread men and brought them to the cottage. She's sitting with him for a few minutes while I fulfil my promise to deliver your book.'

Josh looked around the parlour and burst out laughing.

'Good gracious!' he exclaimed, his eyes travelling round the room, taking in pictures propped haphazardly against every piece of furniture in the room.

'I'll move those from the chair,' she said, picking up two canvasses and moving them elsewhere.

'What's happening, Tessa?' he asked.

'Sorry about the mess. I'm busy sorting out some of my old stuff. Would you like a drink? It'll have to be either coffee or tea. I don't have anything stronger to offer you,' she said shortly.

Looking perplexed, Josh answered quietly, 'Coffee will be fine.'

Tessa stomped into the kitchen. So why had she asked him in? Sure, he'd given her his book, no doubt expected her to be impressed by his amazing talent, and it would be good. He seemed to have a flair for doing things exceptionally well. Obviously charismatic, a huge success with the ladies and, in Grandma's parlance, a bit of a charmer.

Well, she was not so easily impressed with his type as some might be, and after his public performance in Newcastle today, if he for one moment thought she would ever act as his voluptuous redhead did today, make a similar exhibition of herself, he did not know Tessa Robson!

'Your studio is taking shape. Have you a moving-in date?' Josh asked, casually walking into the tiny kitchen, looking at her, touching her face and tucking a few wayward strands of hair behind her ear.

'What's wrong? You're upset about something, Tess.'

Taking a deep breath, she put coffee and cream on a tray, opened a box of biscuits, selected a few and put them on a plate, determined not to give him the satisfaction of knowing why she felt as tetchy as she did.

'It's not like you. Something has made you jumpy. Maybe a hitch with the studio?' he suggested, looking concerned.

'According to my father, the builders are on schedule,' she answered, successfully side-stepping his more personal question which she considered none of his business anyway.

Looking at his watch a few minutes later, Josh drained his coffee cup.

'It's time I was going. Thanks for the coffee, Tess.'

'Thanks for the book,' she reciprocated. 'But wait, hold on just a minute. I bought something in town for James today,' she said, halfway to her bedroom for a large carrier bag which she brought to Josh who peeked inside then, one by one, picked out the contents.

'A yellow sou'wester, yellow oilskin and yellow wellies?'

'I hope he likes them. Let me know if they're a bit big.'

'Thank you and sure, I'll let you know,' he answered with a warm smile.

6

Early the following morning, Tessa was standing at the parlour window, brooding on the subject for her next drawing when she spotted the two figures. The tiny one was James, kitted out in his new yellow ensemble bringing an immediate smile to her lips. The tall figure of his father elicited no more than a passing acknowledgement of his presence.

Tessa ran to the door and opening it said, 'Wow! You look smashing, James, a real, honest-to-goodness fisherman.'

A chubby finger pointed to his sou'wester.

'A hat, Tessa.'

'And a very snazzy hat it is, and if you haven't had breakfast yet, you could have yours with me.'

Unsure, James looked hopefully at his father.

127

'It's very early to call, but the minute he saw your present he had to put it on and then come to show you. You must thank Tessa, James.'

'He can do that in the kitchen. We'll have boiled eggs, toasted soldiers and when the sun comes out, we'll go down to the river, just you and me. I have no objection to dating fishermen if your father doesn't mind his son consorting with designing females, James.'

Tessa felt the steady gaze of Josh's dark-blue eyes on her.

'You'll want to get on with your work. Don't be fooled by his angelic looks. My son can be quite a distracting handful.'

A chip off the old block came to Tessa's mind as James said excitedly, 'See the ducks and swans and the boat, Tessa?'

'Yes. We'll take a camera and two sketch books, one for you, one for me and we'll let your father get on with his scribbling today.'

'And feed the ducks,' James reminded her.

Josh smiled at her.

'This is a generous gesture above and beyond.'

'With selfish undertones. As soon as I saw him in this morning, I wanted to paint James. I think the sou'wester did it. And it's going to be another warm, sunny day.'

When, hours later, Tessa laid her sketchbook to one side and looked at her watch, she couldn't believe it was almost teatime. They had missed lunch and James must be hungry. His father would think she couldn't be trusted to look after his son, she thought, speedily packing her bag.

'We're going home now, Skipper. Time to tie up the boat, and go for lunch,' she announced in her best nautical voice.

James looked at her shyly.

'This is for you.'

She had shown him how to string daisies together in one of their quieter

129

moments, but had no idea this was what he was making as he sat quietly in the boat on the grassy riverbank.

'It's like a beautiful crown, James. If it's for me, I'll be a queen.'

'A fairy queen with flowers in your hair,' he said as she kneeled in front of her young friend, trying to keep her face as straight as possible.

Wondering what had delayed them, Josh sauntered across the estate and, nearing the river, came upon the moving sight of Tessa on her knees, her hair shining in the sunlight, a garland of daisies being placed on her head by an extraordinarily studious James.

The beauty of the scene momentarily reminded Josh of the heartbreaking void his wife's death had left. Whereas he had found a way of coping with his loss, helping James to overcome the shock and sudden emptiness in his young life had been, and to some degree still was, something he struggled with. Yet, however hard he tried, there was little he could do to replicate the warmth and tenderness of a mother's love for her child.

'You look much too engrossed to think of anything as mundane as food, but there's a stack of ham sandwiches beginning to curl at the corners in the cottage,' he called, striding towards them.

'Daddy, look at Tessa. She's a queen,' James shouted.

Grinning self-consciously, Tessa rose to her feet, caught a glimpse of her crumpled shorts and be-spattered T-shirt and sought comfort in the knowledge that while the father might think her a peasant, in his son's eyes, she was a queen. She raised her hands to her hair and made sure her crown of daisies was secure.

'I don't know about you, James Maitland, but those sandwiches sound good to me.'

Shortly afterwards, James was almost falling asleep at the table.

When Josh picked him up in his arms and said, 'Time for tired boys to have a nap,' there wasn't the slightest murmur of objection from James only a tired smile and the subdued plea, 'Tessa won't leave me, Daddy?'

Josh glanced at Tessa who saw the pain in his eyes.

'Tessa's a friend, James, and friends live in their own houses.'

'But how about me tucking you into bed?' Tessa said, following James into the bedroom, thinking the child's few words had been simple, so easy to misconstrue.

Yet it was not so much the words as the plaintive little voice and heartbreakingly sad expression that told Tessa what lay behind the child's fear. The sudden loss of his mother had left James a lonely, insecure child.

'Tell you what, James. You know I live at The Lodge and, because we're such good friends, you are specially invited to come and see me anytime. No other person is allowed to do that, just you.'

He smiled at her and his little arms stole around her neck. Tessa hugged him to her and kissed his cheek, at the same time trying to blink away tears that suddenly threatened to engulf her.

'Come and finish your lunch. I'll make some fresh coffee,' Josh said.

'Thanks, Josh,' she answered huskily. 'You have a beautiful little boy.'

'And I think my beautiful little boy is half in love with his dark-haired, blue-eyed girlfriend.'

'Ah, the story of my life. And fifty per cent is so niggardly, neither one thing nor the other,' she added light-heartedly.

'Some of us learn to settle for a lot less,' he replied quietly.

His comment would have elicited sympathy had Tessa not recalled his Newcastle clinch with the stunning redhead.

'I took some snapshots of James today. They should be good, but look, it's high time I left and let you get on with your writing.'

'You don't have to go. I've done well today, thanks to you. I don't usually get such a long, uninterrupted run.'

She stood up.

'Good. I enjoyed his company and thanks for lunch which, you might've noticed, I also appreciated.'

'And I saw how much James loved being with you,' he said, getting to his feet, reaching and taking her hand in his and gazing steadily at her. 'And in your case I have to agree, Tess. Fifty per cent is pathetically half-hearted,' he said softly, raising her hand to his lips.

In the days that followed, from the bright light of early morning to the first evening shadows, Tessa worked on the paintings she had chosen for Giles Shepherd to see. The night before his visit, she went to bed tired, but pleasantly so after completing the task she had set herself.

Tessa was up early the next day, smartly dressed for business in a silver-grey trouser suit, when the dark green Jaguar pulled up. After stopping to take a good look at the large, imposing studio nearing completion,

Giles Shepherd knocked at her door.

'Good morning, Tessa. I've been admiring your studio.'

'Good morning. It would've been good to have it up and running these past few days instead of working here to the accompaniment of carpenter's saws, hammers and drills,' she complained, then laughed at his pained expression. 'But come and tell me what you think of my latest masterpiece, or perhaps you would like a cup of coffee and something to eat first?'

'I've had breakfast, thank you, and can't wait to see the masterpiece.'

So he had a sense of humour. Tessa fancied it would come in handy today, maybe even help her through this nerve-shredding ordeal. But during the next half hour, there were no jokes, not as much as a question asked by the art gallery owner as he walked round the parlour closely inspecting, lifting the occasional picture off the wall, holding it to a brighter light for a few moments before replacing it. Eventually he smiled at her.

'Who is the little dark-haired boy?'

'That's James. He lives here, on the estate.'

'It's such a charming picture. I thought he might be yours.'

'Mine? But I'm not married,' she explained, immediately cringing at the naïvety of such a statement in an age of one-parent families.

'It is charming, Tessa. So, together with your six smaller drawings, I would like to take your water colour of little James and the rowing boat with me, the Delphinium oil and The Market Place, if that's all right with you?'

To Tessa, this was a dream come true and she didn't know whether to laugh or cry. She felt like dancing and singing and as for asking if it was all right to take three of her pictures with him, heavens above, she wanted to throw her arms around Giles Shepherd's neck and kiss him!

'Yes, of course,' she replied breathlessly. 'I'm pleased your journey hasn't been in vain. Actually, I'm delighted you think my work worthy of your London gallery.'

'I can assure you it is, but come and show me your impressive-looking studio. It looks just about completed.'

Even in its unfinished state, Tessa had to agree her studio was an impressive building.

'The electricians have almost completed their work, in fact everything will be done before the promised completion date, thanks to my father who has a way of getting things done. You'll see what I mean when you meet him.'

'Cressy Slater told me he was a detective inspector here in King's Denton when he inherited the estate. That's quite a career change.'

'It was a tremendous jolt. Everything was in a sorry state of disrepair at that time and poor old Cecilia Calvert-Denton left precious little money, but my parents somehow managed to keep the estate intact,' Tessa explained, surprised to feel the touch of his hand on hers.

'No rings, I see, but I can't believe there isn't a young man in your life. Let me guess. You left them all heartbroken in Paris.'

Tessa laughed.

'All the best ones were spoken for,' she answered glibly, quickly glancing at her watch. 'My parents were hoping you would have lunch at The Hall before leaving, but they'll understand if you're pushed for time.'

'After hearing so much about your family from our mutual friend, I would like to meet them.'

As they walked up the drive, Tessa relaxed a little and began to feel more comfortable in Giles Shepherd's easy-going company.

'No meaningful relationship at all, Tessa?'

She shook her head.

'And what about you?' she ventured bravely.

'Divorced eight years ago.'

'I'm sorry. That must be a painful experience, particularly where children are involved.'

'Strange that at the time of the split I was glad we didn't have children, yet now I bitterly regret not having a family,' he confided thoughtfully. 'Stranger still that I've never spoken of that regret to anyone. Could be the result of all this beauty around me in one gulp,' he added, gazing earnestly at Tessa as they strolled towards The Hall in the warm, midday sun.

Her parents waved to Tessa and her guest from the front of the house. After the introductions were over, full of his usual bonhomie, Ben invited Giles into The Hall.

'I understand you're hurrying off to London after lunch, but Sally and I hope you'll come back for the grand opening of Tessa's studio in a couple of weeks. It should be quite a party.'

If the invitation surprised her guest, Tessa was equally taken aback. It was the first she had heard of a party and was beginning to wonder what else her parents had up their secretive sleeves.

'Good idea. The more who know you

have such a gifted daughter, the better. Getting people interested in a new talent is more than half the battle, and thank you, I would love to come,' Giles replied.

When Calvert breezed in, lunch had already started.

'Sorry I'm late, Mother, Dad. Pleased to meet you, Giles. Hi, sis.'

Long since convinced her brother could charm the birds off the trees, Calvert's cheerful greeting made Tessa smile and consider it small wonder Mel Sinclair was still in love with him after all these years.

With Giles about to leave for London and Calvert for a hearing at the country court, lunch was not the leisurely affair either Sally or Ben had envisaged. When Cal apologised for his hurried departure, on impulse, with a mumbled excuse, Tessa left the table and caught up with him in the hall.

'Hold on a minute, Cal. Tell me about Josh Maitland's redhead.'

'A redhead? Well, it wouldn't surprise

me. He's a good-looking guy and women go for that strong, silent type. What's she like?'

'In her late twenties, smart, sexy-looking, probably lives in Newcastle.'

'Sounds Josh's type, but she's new to me. Sorry, sis, but I must dash.'

Although Cal hadn't heard of the beautiful redhead, he had made it sound as if that female wasn't the only one in Josh's life, Tessa mused.

Later, Giles took Tessa's hand and thanked her.

'I'm most impressed with your studio and look forward to seeing it finished, but I'll phone before then and be here for your party.'

'Thank you, Giles, and I hope your exhibition is a huge success.'

Before stepping into his gleaming Jaguar, he hesitated for the briefest of moments, turned back and gazed at her before gently brushing his lips across her cheek.

'Take care of yourself, Tessa,' he said softly.

She stood outside The Lodge lost in thought as she watched the car leave the drive and only moved when she heard her mother's voice.

'Tessa, what a charming man, and so distinguished looking.'

'It's the grey hair, Mother. Does it every time.'

'Yes, but it's prematurely grey, Tessa. If I'm any judge, Giles Shepherd's not even in his forties.'

'More to the point, he knows the art business,' Tessa said. 'After he took an age to go through my little exhibition, without any hesitation he picked the three pictures I had chosen as most likely.'

'It's all very exciting for you, Tessa, and your father is thrilled.'

'But I wish he'd told me about this studio party.'

'Oh, it was meant to be a big surprise for you when the time came, dear, but we realised you were sure to find out about it when you heard the delivery vans and cars coming through the big gates.'

Tessa burst out laughing, readily believing it would be as her father had forecast — quite a party.

It was after midnight that night when Tessa finished Josh's book, laid it aside and snuggled down in her bed, her mind on how she had enjoyed it and how full of admiration she was for the author.

Just before she'd left The Hall, Molly Howard had asked if she would drop a box of special cookies off for James on her way home. Without thinking, she had agreed. Later, Tessa had second thoughts, and decided she couldn't call at Briar Rose Cottage with a tin of biscuits in her hand. She didn't want Joshua Maitland running away with the idea that she would use the flimsiest of excuses to see him. While it might be good for his ego to have two women vying for his attention, placing herself in such a pathetically tacky position was not her style.

Nonetheless, his book had to be returned and all the face-saving ideas in

143

the world wouldn't get the box of cookies to James. She also had to face the possibility that, if he was serious about the woman she had seen him with in Newcastle, she could soon lose James as well as his father.

Opening her eyes the next morning, Tessa's lips slowly curled into a smile. The knock on her door was not the brass lion rapping, but sounded more like little knuckles to her. Grabbing her dressing-gown, she opened the door to James who smiled his wide, happy smile.

'I come to see you, Tessa.'

'So I see,' she replied, quickly bending to his height. 'How about a kiss with arms?'

'I do those,' Josh intervened, appearing as if from nowhere, in time to see his son put his arms round his sleepy-looking girlfriend's neck and kiss her prettily flushed cheek.

'And at every available opportunity, I've no doubt,' Tessa said curtly.

She looked down at her bare feet and

favourite old dressing-gown and wished there was a big, deep hole nearby to crawl into.

'Please come in, Josh, and if James would like some breakfast, that's fine, but you must excuse me for a few minutes,' she said, disappearing into the bathroom for a quick shower, then diving into a clean shirt, shorts and plimsolls.

'Right. Eggs, bacon and toast then,' she said, her hair still wet, but feeling readier to face the day.

'We've had breakfast, Tessa, but cook yours and I'll make the coffee,' Josh offered.

'You're on. There's milk and some of Mrs Howard's cookies especially for you, James.'

'Did you get a chance to read my book yet? I saw you had company yesterday. Well, what I saw was the flashy Jaguar in your drive and assumed the rest.'

'Yes, I read your book and thoroughly enjoyed the story, even if I thought the female, Chloe, a bit wimpish. I was going to return it today.'

'I'll be interested to hear why you consider the heroine a wimp,' Josh said, pouring the coffee.

Tessa took her breakfast from the toaster and joined him at the table.

'For one thing, she was altogether too sugary sweet. Look what happened when she discovered there was another woman in his life. Instead of telling him in no uncertain words that it was make-your-mind-up time, what did doormat Chloe do?'

'So you wouldn't have forgiven my hero's single indiscretion?'

'Chloe should've given him his marching orders.'

Josh burst out laughing.

'Then there would've been no book, Tess.'

She laughed with him.

'True, and that would've been a great pity. I enjoyed reading it and think the author must be a really talented guy.'

Some moments later Josh topped her

coffee up, before asking, 'Was yesterday's caller an old friend?'

'Giles? Hardly a friend at all. Yesterday was our second business meeting. He's an art gallery owner and took three of my pictures to show in his next collection. One of them was of James and the boat,' she said, smiling at her young visitor.

'A London gallery, eh? That's great news, Tess. Congratulations. I can see we'll soon have to push the boat out for our celebrated local artist.'

'Apparently, my father already has that well in hand. I've just heard he's planning a big party for the official opening of the studio. I hope you'll be able to come.'

'Have you fixed a date?'

'I'm leaving all that in Dad's hands. As well as thoroughly enjoying the project, he is also footing the bill.'

'I'll look forward to it, and I guess if your father's running the show, it'll be the social event of the year,' he said with a low chuckle. 'But, look, we're taking up your whole morning. Time to go, James.'

'No, Tessa,' James pleaded, looking close to tears.

'Well, I suppose James and I could clear away the dishes, make my bed and tidy up generally before I bring him back to the cottage.'

Josh shook his head, smiled at her and said, 'Who was decrying wimpish females a few minutes ago?'

'Yes, but this is different. The young gentleman we're talking about now is James Maitland, and he's my special friend.'

'You win,' he said softly, running his hand over her hair. 'Still wet. Make sure you dry it before going out or you'll catch your death. James and I won't be here to keep our eyes on you next week, Tess. I have an appointment in London.'

'And James? You're taking James to London?'

'He'll stay with a friend of ours in Newcastle, won't you, James? You're going to stay with Rusty.'

'Rusty,' James chipped in gleefully. 'In Newcastle, Tessa.'

'Wow! That sounds wonderful,' she found herself saying, not feeling half as cheerful as she sounded, barely needing to put two and two together to know Josh's friend Rusty and the glamorous redhead had to be one and the same woman.

What was not so instantly recognisable was the depth of their friendship. Josh must know and trust her implicitly to leave little James in her care. It had to be a much closer relationship than she had envisaged.

7

If asked, Tessa would have stated categorically that she had not a jealous bone in her body, but then that other hackneyed phrase about there being a first time for everything was a sobering thought.

The one bright and exciting spot on her horizon was the completion of the wonderful studio. Even if it was possible to string the right words together to thank her parents, it would never be enough yet, if there was a way to repay their unstinting generosity and help to kick-start her career, she would find it.

Nearby, the persistent hammering and noisy voices came, not from her studio today, but the gang of workmen struggling to erect what looked to Tessa like the biggest marquee she had ever seen.

'What d'you think of it, Tess?' her

father remarked.

'Did it have to be the biggest marquee on the planet?'

'That's the size you need if you want a good-sized dance floor in it.'

Tessa shook her head resignedly. What could she say? With the best of intentions, Ben Robson did things his way. As usual, there would be no argument. Her dear, kind and caring father was a law unto himself.

'I see Josh is still away. Have you heard from him yet?' he asked.

'He told me he had business in London,' she replied, puzzled that her father should ask her about his return.

Why should she hear from Josh Maitland? For all she knew, he could be living it up in Newcastle with Rusty, his latest conquest.

'Right, Tessa. All the invitations have gone out for the studio opening and I've included any Newcastle people connected with the art world. Giles Shepherd says you need the right connections.'

'And I'm sure he's right. Giles knows a lot of people in the business and says he'll be here early to introduce me to his Newcastle associates.'

Ben glanced at his daughter's old, paint-spotted pullover that looked four sizes too big, her old, washed-out jeans, scruffy trainers and suddenly roared with laughter. She waited patiently for his laugh to subside.

'What's the joke, Dad?'

'All your mother and Grandma can talk about is what they'll wear next Friday and just look at you.'

Tessa's short laugh followed her father's.

'What's wrong with this outfit? I thought something like this would make me stand out in the crowd, look different, sort of avant-garde.'

'Oh, it'll do that all right, Tess,' Ben suggested, looking concerned.

'Don't worry, I'm one up on Mum and Grandma. They don't have my little black dress which is French, even more elegant and sophisticated than this outfit,' Tessa teased, reaching up to peck his cheek.

At that moment, her father's hand gripped her arm for what seemed to Tessa like support, and staring at him, she noticed his pallor.

'Daddy? Are you all right? Come into The Lodge and sit down,' she said shakily, suddenly cold and afraid.

When she put a cup of tea in his hand later, Tessa saw with relief that his colour was back to normal and he seemed more like his old self again.

'So, how long is it since you've had a medical check-up?' she asked.

'Why would I have a medical examination when I've never had a day's illness in my life?'

'All that proves is that you've been lucky so far, Daddy. But if Mum has to call a doctor out to you, you might've left it too late,' Tess told him.

'You won't worry your mother about a little bout of indigestion, Tess? That's all it was, y'know,' he stressed.

'I won't if you promise to see Dr

Chisholm soon.'

'For a slip of a girl, Tessa Robson, you are quite a formidable character.'

She glanced up at her father's dear face and said gently, 'I had a fairly formidable and very pushy teacher, Daddy.'

Ben gave a short laugh, drank his tea in one quick gulp and, rising to his feet, ruffled Tessa's hair.

'That's all it was, angel. I've eaten something that didn't agree with me,' he remarked, bringing any further talk about his chest pain to an abrupt end.

Automatically knowing her father would object strongly to the idea of being escorted home, she watched him cross the park, tall, straight, but today she sensed a swagger of defiance in his stride. Commonsense told her that if he wasn't feeling well, being near her mother was the best place for him. And who better than a one-time ward sister?

When he was out of sight, her thoughts swung to Josh Maitland. She looked for a plausible reason, any reason, why he had stayed away longer than originally intended. Understandably she missed little James, but hadn't bargained for feeling as she did about Josh's long absence. There was no pleasure in trying to analyse those feelings when his interest was focused relentlessly on another woman.

It was growing dark and Tessa was concentrating on carefully choosing the best of her pictures for the long south wall of her studio when she heard a gentle tapping. With a sudden rush of happiness, she flew to the door.

'Hello, James,' she said softly, kneeling down, delighted to see him.

'I been to the seaside, Tessa, and this is for you,' he said, offering her a large stick of peppermint rock.

'Wow! Thanks, James, it's my favourite, and the biggest stick of rock I've ever seen. Someone will have to help me eat it. I wonder who?' Tessa asked, momentarily ignoring Josh, watching James grinning from ear to ear, his head nodding, agreeing to help her solve the problem.

From the child's happy face, she glanced at Josh standing beside his son, his eyes steadfastly on her. Tessa straightened up.

'Hi, Josh,' she said nervously. 'Please come in or have you just arrived and want to settle in? What's this about a holiday at the seaside?'

'A completely out-of-the-blue holiday. When I got back from London, we were whisked off to Seahouses to a friend's cottage and I felt they'd been so kind to take James, I had no choice but to go along with their plans. James has had a wonderful time, but I missed this place.'

'I suppose you would find writing almost impossible in a busy seaside place,' she suggested, determined to steer well clear, not remotely hint at the distraction the gorgeous Rusty would be for a dedicated writer.

'Totally. I didn't even think of it, and you guessed right, Tess. We've just arrived and it's time for this fella's bath and his own bed. I must get him back into some sort of routine before school starts.'

'It's good to see you back and you're coming to my studio party?'

'Wouldn't miss it,' he replied, taking her face in his hands and, bending, his lips touched hers. 'I missed you, Tess,' he murmured.

Despite her state of complete bewilderment, Tessa sensed James looking up at her.

'Can I stay with you, Tessa?'

Taking a deep breath, she cleared her throat.

'You can call and see me tomorrow, James, but it's time for your bath now. So, after you've had a long sleep you can come tomorrow and we'll go to The Hall and say hello to everybody.'

Collapsing into a chair after they had gone, Tessa put her hands to her flushed cheeks, warning herself it had not been a peck on the cheek. Josh had kissed her, possibly for no other reason than he was delighted to be back where he could write in peace. She certainly would not be lured into believing a single kiss meant anything of any significance to a man like Josh. She had watched Mel over the years and seen the heartbreak lying in store for a girl loving a man, hoping that one day he would love her in return.

At close quarters and since her early teens she had witnessed Melanie's absolute, unquestioning devotion to Calvert. Mel knew he had girlfriends, and that while he cared for her, they had been so close since early childhood, he thought of her as his other sister. Consequently, in silence and for years her dear friend had suffered the pangs of unrequited love.

'What's more,' Tessa mumbled to herself, 'I've always suspected her love for Cal was the real motivation for cutting herself off, choosing dangerous assignments abroad, and not solely her avowed love of more stimulating journalism.'

The following morning, with the final preparations for the studio on her mind, Tessa walked towards the marquee, thinking the jumbo-sized canvas tent incongruous in its serene parkland setting. But at the same time she was pleasantly surprised by its spacious, airy interior and she couldn't help but admire the polished-wood floor for dancing.

When her phone bleeped she hurried out of the marquee, surprised to hear her mother's worried voice.

'Tessa, your father says he had a sharp bout of indigestion yesterday and you insisted he rested a while. Tell me exactly what happened, dear.'

'More or less what he told you. He had a sharp pain, grabbed my arm and for a few minutes his colour was unusual. I panicked, thought he should sit down and no matter that Daddy thought you would be worried, I'd made up my mind to tell you today.'

'Well, Tessa, I'll make an appointment with Dr Chisholm immediately and your father won't like it, but he has me to deal with now, so you can stop worrying, pet. Everything's ready for tomorrow night's party. Your grandma's already here, has brought every piece of jewellery she owns with her, fiercely determined to outshine us all, as usual.'

Tessa was still laughing when she heard Matt Henderson call to her.

'Your father tells me you need extra fittings, Tessa. Come and show me where and how many.'

Tessa smiled at her father's multi-skilled right-hand man and felt a twinge of guilt for taking him from his estate work. They were in the studio when a little head peeped round the partially-open door.

'Come in and sit quietly until Mr Henderson has finished his work, James, then we'll go to The Hall. Did your daddy bring you?' she asked.

'He did,' Josh replied from the doorway, 'but I can see you're busy.'

'Josh, before you go, would you do me a favour? There are six framed pictures propped up against the sofa in the parlour . . . '

'She's worse than her father, this one, Josh. Always was a little miss bossy boots,' Matt said, laughing at Tessa's indignant expression.

When the last of her pictures was in place, she looked round her studio.

'That's it, finished at last. What d'you think, Josh?' she said.

'It looks superb. You'll enjoy working in this bright atmosphere, although it could be lonely working indoors on your own.'

'Peaceful, you mean, away from all distractions.'

'So, with everything ready, all your building problems solved, you have nothing to think about except the great time you'll have tomorrow.'

Tessa didn't reply. If there was something weighing on her mind, she wasn't prepared to discuss it with anyone, least of all Josh.

'Well, James, are you ready for your walk across the park?'

James jumped to his feet in a flash.

'Thanks for taking him, Tess. I need to go into King's Denton but I'll be back in an hour to pick him up.'

* * *

The first of the cars and delivery vans arrived as Tessa was having her breakfast the next morning and they continued throughout the day. She was hoping Melanie would make it but neither she nor her parents had heard from her for over a week, but if it was at all possible to get here this evening, Tessa knew Mel would make it.

Later, reflected in a long mirror, was an elegantly-dressed, young lady Tessa hardly recognised. Gone was her old, paint-splattered shirt and jeans, and in their place was the chic, little black dress she had bought in a reckless moment in St Germain for just such an occasion as this.

'Not bad,' she murmured.

Tessa laughed quietly to herself as

she slipped into her coat.

The Hall was a blaze of lights and when Molly Howard took her coat, Tessa saw she was excited.

'Everything is going beautifully, Tessa. There's dinner here in The Hall for family, close friends and people like Cressida Slater and Mr Shepherd,' she said breathlessly.

'Has Giles Shepherd arrived yet?'

'He's talking to your grandma in the drawing-room.'

Molly suddenly dropped her voice to a conspiratorial whisper.

'The buffet supper for all your young friends will be served in the marquee later and I've heard the band is a really good one to dance to.'

'You'll know when you join us in the marquee later.'

'I can't, Tessa. I promised I'd stay the night with James. Josh was invited to dinner, but would rather stay with James until dinner's over when I can go there. Look, Tessa, your father's trying to attract your attention.'

The moment Tessa walked into the drawing-room, she was overwhelmed by the warmth of her reception and was instantly surrounded by family and friends, a happy, noisy gathering, every one of them a well-wisher, all dressed for the occasion in their party best.

'Hi, beautiful,' her father teased, looking smart, younger than his fifty-five years and dispelling any doubts she'd had earlier about his health.

'You look lovely tonight,' Giles said, putting a glass of iced tonic on a nearby table for her. 'Cal told me you'd prefer that.'

'Thanks, Giles, but tell me, how did your show go?'

'Your work was greatly admired and, as I suspected, things went well. I wish you'd been there, Tessa.'

Giles pulled an envelope out of his pocket and passed it to her.

'Your cheque,' he said quietly.

Tessa stared at it in wide-eyed disbelief.

'You sold them? All of them? How fantastic!'

164

Giles was still nodding his head and smiling indulgently at her when, with a spontaneous expression of gratitude, she flung her arms around his neck.

'You've really made my evening, Giles Shepherd.'

When, self-consciously, Tessa quickly glanced round, she saw her moment of madness was being thoroughly enjoyed by everyone looking on, including Josh Maitland who, with Melanie, had just walked into the room.

'Mel, this is great. I knew you'd manage to get here somehow,' Tessa greeted her friend warmly.

'And it looks as if I've arrived just in time for the floor show,' she quipped, looking at Giles. 'Misguidedly, I was under the impression Tessa Robson was the shy, retiring type.'

Suddenly remembering her conversation with Molly earlier, Tessa turned to Josh.

'Who is looking after James?'

'He's in the kitchen with Molly and her army of helpers. A brainwave of your mother's with which I was more than happy to go along.'

'Tessa's mother has a natural flair for this sort of thing, always had,' Mel added, smiling at Giles. 'Have you met my parents yet?'

The lights from the studio could be seen from the top of the drive and when the time came, with the unforeseen additional help of a brilliant full moon, the dinner party guests were guided towards the studio and the marquee where the band was already tuning up.

Puzzled, Tessa looked at the Morgan standing in front of The Hall.

'Why did you park your car up here, Josh?'

'There's something in it I've been looking after for you,' he replied mysteriously. 'I'll show you later. Get in and I'll run you to the studio.'

Remaining silent and suspicious, she did as Josh instructed and after stopping the car outside The Lodge, he switched off the engine and turning, he picked up a basket and put it in her lap.

Hesitant, still trying to envisage what he could possibly have been looking after for her, Tessa looked down at the small, partially-open wicker basket. A minuscule black puppy looked up at her, its soulful dark eyes enough to melt the stoniest heart. Tessa gasped, delight suddenly suffusing her face.

'A dog will be company for you when we're not around,' Josh said.

'Isn't she beautiful, Josh? But she must feel restricted in such a confined space. I'll put her in The Lodge.'

'She's a he, Tess,' he told her, seeing how completely captivated she was and reckoning he could confidently stop thinking himself crazy for giving her such an individual, very personal present.

'Thank you, Josh. I do appreciate him. Does he have a name?'

'They called him Charlie at the dog pound.'

'Well, Charlie, you'll never go back there. You have a proper home now and, what's more, a whole park of your own to play in.'

Thoughts of her little black spaniel stayed with Tessa as people filed into the studio, but uppermost in her mind was the extraordinary thoughtfulness of Josh. And he was right, Charlie would be good company, yet Josh's gift could never replace the void his eventual departure from the estate would create.

Giles Shepherd's attention was totally focused on the pictures Tessa had on display in the studio, fielding questions and making himself useful.

'He is very attractive, Tessa, charming, sophisticated, but with my luck, married,' Mel said to her friend.

'Married and divorced. Mother and Grandma think he's wonderful, so join the club, Mel,' Tessa said, then more seriously, 'And keep your fingers crossed for me. I've sunk everything into it. All my time, hopes and dreams are tied up in this venture of mine.'

'Come on, Tess, this is not like you. What's the worst that can happen? That people don't like your work? Giles knows the art world and he's very impressed, and Cressy has just bought those two pastels of leopard cubs and she's another professional.'

'You're right, Mel, I'm being a pain. It's time we joined the others in the marquee. Grandma is already there.'

'Probably jitterbugging with the best-looking guy around.'

Tessa was still laughing when Josh appeared.

'One tired pup safely sleeping in a makeshift bed in your kitchen.'

'And I was thinking that Charlie could become a fine watchdog, Josh.'

'Oh, he'd scare any intruder witless, I reckon,' he agreed.

After the buffet supper, the tables were quickly cleared, the five-piece band struck up a lively tune and the dancing was in full swing when Tessa, Melanie, Cal, Josh and Giles walked into the marquee to join the noisy, boisterous crowd who appeared to be enjoying themselves enormously. When the tune changed to a slower, more romantic tempo, Josh tugged her hand gently.

'Let's dance, Tess.'

Without a word, she was in his arms, all doubts and worries about her precipitous leap into the art world and the nagging off-chance that Josh might soon leave the estate, all slipped from her mind.

'Our first dance together,' Josh murmured, holding her close and, as their eyes met and held, Tessa knew this was where she wanted to be, and, whatever the future held, she could not deny her love for Josh Maitland.

'You're frowning and very quiet,' he said guardedly. 'Tonight's been such a huge success in every way, you can't be dissatisfied or unhappy. D'you want to tell me about it?'

'It's late and I've had a hectic day. With so much dependent upon the success of tonight, of people turning up, seeing the studio and liking my work, it has been a surprisingly emotional experience, Josh.'

'Giles has been a big help, I hear.'

'He has been such a kind and good friend. That he liked my work gave a huge boost to my flagging confidence, then to have a professional art dealer offer help and advice seemed heaven-sent.'

Josh lowered his head and his lips touched her hair.

'Don't get too enthusiastic about Giles or you'll make James jealous,' he said softly.

Hours later, when the band had packed up and departed, her grandma called it a day and Giles took Melanie home, much to Calvert's annoyance. Before her guests drifted away, Tessa thanked everyone for coming and making the evening such an unqualified success. Scanning the dance floor, she gave Josh a wry smile.

'Looks as if everyone had a good time,' she commented, ankle-deep in floor-strewn streamers, deflated blue, white and silver balloons and general end-of-party debris.

'It's time I took you home, Tess.'

'To my ferocious guard dog,' she began, and made him laugh. 'I appreciate your thoughtfulness and your help tonight.'

'Teamwork,' he said, taking her face in his hands and lightly brushing his lips lightly over hers. 'I know you have something on your mind, Tess, but now is not the time, so we'll talk tomorrow.'

'And you think talking will solve my problem?'

'Maybe not, but it could resolve mine,' he answered obscurely, taking her hand. 'The party's over, Tess, and it's high time you were fast asleep.'

Tessa smiled. For a moment he might have been talking to James, but why that thought should suddenly bring her close to tears was 'way beyond her comprehension. Josh ran his hand caressingly down her hair.

'Good-night, Tess. Sleep well and we'll talk tomorrow.'

And he was right. She'd had a long,

exciting day, enjoyed it enormously and if there were a few hiccoughs on her horizon, as Grandma was fond of saying. 'There's nothing like a good night's sleep for getting things back in perspective, pet.' She stood watching Josh walk towards the park.

8

An immediate and striking change in the weather in a mere twenty-four hours astonished Tessa. A cold, blustery wind picked up strength and on her way to The Hall for lunch, Tessa didn't envy the men struggling to take down the marquee.

When Molly opened the door, Tessa said, 'You were right, the band was exceptionally good last night.'

'And so was little James. When you think of what that little bairn has suffered, Tessa, it's heartbreaking. He was so good, fell asleep as soon as his head touched the pillow. But when Josh marries again, he'll have another mother to take care of him, poor lamb.'

'Yes,' Tessa responded thoughtfully, hearing female voices and quickly making for the drawing-room.

'Tessa, what a party! I don't know

when I've enjoyed myself more.'

'Everyone seemed to enjoy it, Grandma. Does Daddy know they've already started dismantling the marquee?'

Ben Robson laughed as she walked into the room.

'They could be blown to kingdom come in this gale,' Ben managed to say before suddenly, he slapped a flattened hand against his chest.

He stared at Sally, looking bewildered.

'The pain, Sal,' he gasped before collapsing to the floor.

'I'll see to this,' her mother commanded. 'Call for an ambulance.'

Tessa rushed for the hall phone. Shakily, she dialled emergency, telling herself to act as her mother would. Her father was having a heart attack and she must cope with it, stay calm and controlled for their sake.

'We're going to the hospital, Ben,' her mother was saying when Tessa returned to the room after making the phone call.

'It'll be here any minute. I'll get his pyjamas, slippers and stuff packed and follow in your car.'

The speed of events that afternoon was something Tessa looked back on later that evening with a mixture of amazement and gratitude to the ambulance men and medical staff for their speed in getting her father into the heart unit without wasting a second of valuable, lifesaving time.

Her grandma looked worried when she returned to The Hall and suddenly, to Tessa, very frail. Tessa understood how much she loved her big son-in-law, had always considered him a fine man and been delighted when her daughter had married Ben Robson.

'How is he, Tessa?' she asked anxiously.

'Too early to say, Grandma. They're doing a lot of tests, so it'll take a few days. There's nothing we can do at the moment except wait.'

'Your mother will stay with him tonight?'

'Yes, and she wants me to stay here with you tonight, but first I must go to The Lodge. I haven't had a chance to tell you, but Josh gave me a tiny spaniel puppy. He thought I might need company on my busy days in the studio. The thing is, the dear little dog has been alone and completely neglected since lunchtime.'

'Get yourself away then and bring the poor creature back here and let me have a look at him. What's her name?'

Tessa smiled and said, 'It's a boy, Charlie.'

Hurriedly buttoning up her coat, Tess left The Hall guessing that the laughter she heard was young James and felt a twinge of guilt for not phoning Josh this morning to explain what had happened.

'I've been trying to contact you all morning,' Josh snapped, as he appeared. 'You look pale. Are you all right?'

'Sorry, I left my mobile in The Lodge. It's my father, Josh. He's been taken to the hospital and I'm waiting for news from Mother.'

Tessa had as little power to control the unsteadiness of her voice as she had to stem the tears that filled her eyes or the sobs that shook her body. Josh's arms instantly reached out and tugged her close.

'Poor Tessa. Don't cry, Tessa, better soon,' James said, looking up at her, his little face filled with concern.

She took a deep, steadying breath, wiped her fingers across her wet face and said, 'There's something special in The Lodge for you to see, James.'

'Come on, then, let's take Tessa home,' Josh added.

That James would be captivated by the puppy, Josh had foreseen, but when Tessa walked into the kitchen and pointed to Charlie's makeshift bed and his son saw the bundle of black silky fur, and the dark, soulful eyes gazing back at him, Josh saw his little boy was instantly besotted.

'Can I touch him, Tessa?'

'You can, and take him for walks

soon. Dogs love going for walks.'

'I'll take you to the hospital to see your father this evening,' Josh said. 'He could be in intensive care and not allowed visitors, but we'll see. Come here, Tess, I need to talk to you,' he said, walking out of the kitchen.

Warily, she followed him into the parlour.

'I don't think my brain could cope with anything too serious today, Josh.'

'You can either sit or stand, but you will hear me out, Tess,' Josh said crustily. 'Are you in love with Giles Shepherd?'

'And if I was?' she shot back, suddenly annoyed and aware she was shouting. 'What could it possibly have to do with you?'

'It has everything to do with me. I'm in love with you, dammit, and it's been staring you in the face for weeks, but for some reason you keep shying away from me and it's time I knew why.'

Tessa was also trying to control her increasing anger at his arrogance.

'That's quite a revelation, and if I thought you hadn't said something similar to your redheaded Newcastle girlfriend, I might've believed it. Lucky for me I knew about her. Second best has never been good enough for me.'

'Would you care to unravel that for me?'

'How many redheads do you take in your arms and kiss in broad daylight in the middle of Newcastle? And don't deny it. I was there, Josh, and saw you. What's more, are you sure she loves James as she should? I sincerely hope so, for your son is an extremely sensitive child. Is she aware of that?'

The dawning of a smile at the corners of his mouth stopped her.

'The lady you saw me with is my cousin and the wife of a good friend of mine, Tess.'

'And a very accommodating friend he must be to allow another man to kiss his wife in full view of a Newcastle lunchtime crowd.'

'It's true I hugged, kissed and

congratulated her, but she had just told me she was expecting their first child. It was Rusty and my aunt who looked after James when my wife was ill and I'll be eternally grateful to them.'

Tessa had the grace to look shamefaced.

'I'm sorry. It seems I jumped to the wrong conclusion.'

'With both feet,' he murmured with a broad grin.

'Well, it's not Giles Shepherd I'm in love with.'

Suddenly, Tessa was in his arms.

Later, his arm still encircling her waist, he confided, 'I hoped against hope, thought it was asking too much of you to take on a ready-made family, but then, you love James.'

'Can we keep this to ourselves for a while, Josh?'

'We must. I wouldn't want your father to think he's losing his daughter, not the way he must be feeling at the moment.'

Any thought they had about shock

waves was dispelled the minute they walked into the hospital ward and saw Ben sitting up in bed chatting matter-of-factly to his wife about buying a new combine harvester!

'How are you, Daddy?' she asked gently, kissing his cheek.

'I'm fine. I told you there was nothing to worry about. It wasn't my heart at all, just a chest pain. Pull up a chair, Josh. You look surprised.'

'That could be because I fully expected to find you in intensive care.'

'I should've phone you earlier, Tessa,' her mother began apologetically. 'They're keeping your father in tonight for further observation, but we should be home after the results of the tests tomorrow. The good news is they're almost sure it was an angina pain and not something more serious.'

At the sound of Calvert's car the following afternoon, Tessa rushed to the door to welcome her parents home, and after the noise and excitement of hugs, kisses, chatter and laughter, Molly

Howard tugged Tessa's sleeve and asked quietly, 'Have you seen James anywhere?'

'James came over to play with Charlie. He'll be in the courtyard teaching him to beg,' Tessa said lightly, giving an unconcerned shrug.

'I've looked outside and he's definitely not in the courtyard.'

Tessa felt the faintest unease.

'Right, Molly, he knows I'm going back to The Lodge today and that's where he'll be, waiting there for me with Charlie and I'll tell the little toad off for frightening you.'

'Oh, Tessa, don't. James is just an adventurous little boy.'

She reached for her coat and shouted to the family she'd be back soon.

Tessa was mystified when there was neither sight nor sound of James and the puppy. Feeling uneasy, she searched the area of parkland immediately surrounding The Lodge before hurrying on to Josh's cottage.

'I'm looking for James. Is he here?'

she asked Josh casually.

'Molly's keeping an eye on him for an hour or two.'

'She was, but we can't find him anywhere near The Hall and while I assumed he would be at The Lodge, he's not there either.'

'I'll get my jacket on and we'll find him together. Come on, Tessa, you know where all his favourite hiding places are and that's where he'll be, somewhere like Calvert's little boat.'

'You're right, Josh, the boat. Where else?' she said, more to herself, and she would stay cool, determinedly focused until she found him. 'I never was the panicky type and this is certainly not the time to start losing my nerve.'

'Hm?' Josh murmured, busily scanning the stretch of river, lifting the upturned boat. 'There's no sign of him here, Tess. Where next?'

'We'll look around the dovecote on the way back to The Hall. He's probably sitting in the kitchen eating cookies,' she said, trying to bolster her wavering courage.

'You can't find James? He'll be playing with Charlie in the old station wagon in the big stable,' her father suggested, when Tessa told him they were looking for James. 'I'll put my coat on. I'll soon find him.'

'No, Ben,' Josh butted in. 'It's turning cold out there. You've just come out of hospital and should be resting. Tessa and I can manage.'

'A good walk would do me the world of good. Plenty of exercise is what I need, not sitting in a chair for hours on end and it'll be getting dark as well as colder soon,' Ben reminded them, rising to his feet. 'Now, where have you looked so far?'

When Ben set off for the big stable that these days was used as little more than a garage for his old station wagon, Tessa and Josh continued their search, starting again with the courtyard and out-buildings of The Hall. Josh took her hand.

'Don't worry, Tess, he can't be far

away. James,' he yelled at the top of his voice, the call loud and clear.

They stood together waiting and hoping as the sky darkened and the first spots of rain fell, but only the powerful after-effect of Josh's call hung in the evening air. Tessa shivered as the sound of Josh's mobile broke the silence.

'Yes, Ben. I see. We're speeding up our search round The Hall.'

After slipping the phone back in his pocket, he ran his fingers down Tessa's cheek.

'Your father thinks the estate workers would want to help in the search and I think we should be guided by him in this. We need help, Tess.'

'James has to be somewhere. We're just missing something, Josh. Where would he go? What would make a five-year-old suddenly disappear?' Tessa asked, her voice sinking to a choked whisper.

'Charlie slipping his leash and James running after him is an obvious possibility,' Josh suggested, looking desperately for clues.

Tessa shivered.

'What can we do now, Josh?' she asked, a note of despair creeping into her voice. 'Should we look in Downey Cottage? It has been empty and locked up since old Mr Armstrong died. The keys for Downey are hanging in The Hall kitchen.'

'There's not much likelihood of him being there, Tess, not if it's locked, but get the key. It's worth a try.'

The drizzling rain gradually increased to a steady downpour as they ran across the estate in the direction of the two cottages.

'I'll look round the back of Briar Rose again while you unlock Downey and I'll be with you in a few minutes, Tess.'

At least they were doing something. Poor Josh. She had seen how pale he was, how his lips had tightened to a grim line and she could only imagine the state of his mind. She pushed the door wide.

'James. Are you here, James? It's Tessa.'

Dripping wet, Tessa stood in the cottage, feeling numb, her mind a blank, her movements automatic as she pushed herself to keep searching until she found James and Charlie.

How could she ever have believed that Josh had some ulterior motive in sitting guard outside her bedroom door all those years ago and worse, that she had never trusted him since, not entirely. It had taken these long hours of searching together to make her think very differently of the man she loved, how she respected and admired his unflagging, heartbreaking concern for the motherless little boy he loved.

He came into the cottage, strode towards her and, without uttering a sound, took her in his arms and held her head against his chest.

'We'll have to inform the police soon, Josh.'

'Your father will see to that when the time comes, but in the meantime I'm sure you're right about us overlooking something somewhere. We'll go back to The Hall's outbuildings.'

In the gathering gloom, they retraced their tracks, first to scan the courtyard more, search its old stone buildings, then take a closer look in the big stable. When Josh slammed the station wagon doors in disgust at finding it empty, Tessa stood as if turned to stone and stared ahead.

'What's the matter?'

'There was a noise, up there.'

Tessa pointed beyond the wooden rails separating stalls, the one-time homes for the Denton Park estate's working horses.

'In the far corner,' she added in a hushed tone.

Flicking his torch, Josh threw a shaft of light across the stable and, hesitantly, Tessa walked towards what appeared to be bales of hay. Tears of relief and gratitude sprang to her eyes as she gazed at Charlie lying at the feet of James, both sound asleep. Tessa was suddenly engulfed by such an over-whelming feeling of pure happiness, she scarcely felt Josh's steadying hand on the small of her back.

'I must get in touch with your father, tell him to call off the search,' Josh said shakily, turning the torch beam towards his son's rosy face.

James stirred, blinked against the glare of light, slowly opened his eyes and smiled at his father.

Much later that evening, Josh and Tessa were able to piece together the story of how Charlie had run off, with James chasing after him until both boy and puppy, completely exhausted, came upon the open door of the stable where they sought shelter.

'We're lucky to have found them unhurt, Tess, thanks to you and your unwavering perseverance. I know now just how much he means to you.'

'James is a loving little boy and I can easily imagine his mother had a gentle, caring nature.'

'She did and I loved her, Tess, but

you were perhaps my first love,' he said quietly, taking her in his arms.

'I was? Honestly?'

'A lovely, wayward teenager, and the girl of my dreams. My first love and my last,' he vowed, his lips against hers.

THE END

We do hope that you have enjoyed reading this large print book.

Did you know that all of our titles are available for purchase?

We publish a wide range of high quality large print books including:
Romances, Mysteries, Classics
General Fiction
Non Fiction and Westerns

Special interest titles available in large print are:
The Little Oxford Dictionary
Music Book, Song Book
Hymn Book, Service Book

Also available from us courtesy of Oxford University Press:
Young Readers' Dictionary
(large print edition)
Young Readers' Thesaurus
(large print edition)

For further information or a free brochure, please contact us at:
Ulverscroft Large Print Books Ltd.,
The Green, Bradgate Road, Anstey,
Leicester, LE7 7FU, England.
Tel: (00 44) **0116 236 4325**
Fax: (00 44) **0116 234 0205**

Other titles in the
Linford Romance Library:

THREE TALL TAMARISKS

Christine Briscomb

Joanna Baxter flies from Sydney to run her parents' small farm in the Adelaide Hills while they recover from a road accident. But after crossing swords with Riley Kemp, life is anything but uneventful. Gradually she discovers that Riley's passionate nature and quirky sense of humour are capturing her emotions, but a magical day spent with him on the coast comes to an abrupt end when the elegant Greta intervenes. Did Riley love Greta after all?

SUMMER IN
HANOVER SQUARE

Charlotte Grey

The impoverished Margaret Lambart is suddenly flung into all the glitter of the Season in Regency London. Suspected by her godmother's nephew, the influential Marquis St. George, of being merely a common adventuress, she has, nevertheless, a brilliant success, and attracts the attentions of the young Duke of Oxford. However, when the Marquis discovers that Margaret is far from wanting a husband he finds he has to revise his estimate of her true worth.